Jean Lyle
15 Sep 98

THE FINDING OF JASPER HOLT

Grace Livingston Hill

THE FINDING OF
JASPER HOLT

A BARBOUR BOOK

Published by Barbour and Company, Inc.
P.O. Box 719
Uhrichsville, OH 44683

ISBN 1-55748-238-1

Introduction

Where did my mother learn such depth of holy romance as she brought out in her books?

It may have been through bits of confidences here and there, gathered from the young people who were so much a part of her life in our college town.

She was always keen to recognize fineness of character, even in some of the young fellows who had somehow earned the distrust of the villagers. It may be that her unwavering trust in the faithfulness of God steadied her confidence in their earnest professions of faith as she watched them desperately struggling to walk in new, straight paths. Perhaps that confidence gave them, in turn, a hitherto unknown strength of purpose. It may be that in eternity she will find that her Lord used her to draw some of those young pilgrims into a deeper knowledge of Himself.

It is certain that the ideals and high standards she presented in her books have inspired some of her readers to relinquish the uncertain, decaying ways of our modern world and seek for lasting values. I will always be grateful for the uncompromising truth she presented to us.

RUTH LIVINGSTON HILL

THE FINDING OF JASPER HOLT

Chapter 1

Slowly the train rumbled out of the station, gathering speed with every moment, and leaving behind the friendly faces on the platform.

The girl who had just entered the car looked about her in dismay at the rough-looking crowd by whom she was surrounded. It was the last long stretch of her journey now, out on the plains and across the desert, and the porter of the sleeper had refused to let her enter the pullman coach without a pullman ticket. Of course it would be all right when the conductor came, but suppose her brother-in-law had forgotten to telegraph for the reservation and she should have to spend the night in this car?

She slipped into the only vacant seat and sat anxiously awaiting the coming of the conductor, who was nowhere in sight.

For the most part the people about her were rough, stolid men with hard brown faces. Here and there a woman was huddled wearily into a corner of the seat trying to sleep. They were commonplace folk, nearly all of them, and their very ordinariness brought her some measure of assurance, yet she shuddered at the thought of spending her night huddled into a seat, like the other women, with all those men about, free to gaze on her as she slept.

She glanced across the aisle where the seat was turned over and two men faced each other, an old man and a young one. The old man sat just across from her, his coarse stubbly face turned boldly toward her. He had crafty little eyes that intruded with their merest glance, windows out of which coarseness, hate, cruelty and fear alike might look; a sensual loose-hung mouth, and a whole repulsive atmosphere of

9

cunning that made his face seem utterly evil. Insensibly she shrank farther away and looked hurriedly about to see if perchance there might not after all be another vacant seat where she could be entirely out of his range. Then her eyes suddenly met the eyes of his companion who faced her, the young man in the turned-over seat, and she wondered how she could have failed to notice him at once. There was something about his face—perhaps it was the splendid gray eyes that were looking at her so keenly and respectfully, or was it the firm chin and almost stern set of the beautiful lines of lip and brow that gave her confidence in him at once? For there was a strength and beauty in his face such as one seldom sees blended in a man, which marked him at once as being different from others. There was nothing weak nor womanish about him, in spite of the perfect modeling of his features and the clear coloring of his skin. The fine golden-brown hair that rippled back from his forehead like a halo gave the impression of curling out of perverseness rather than from the owner's wish.

He was tall and lean and wiry, yet giving the idea of great strength and fine training. If it had not been for an abnormal gravity and the sternness about his mouth, she would have judged him to be a mere boy, yet there was an air of maturity about him that puzzled her. But his gray eyes met hers kindly, understandingly, as if he knew exactly what she was thinking—all her anxiety—and would let her know that she was safe, that he would see that she was safe! It was with an almost startled feeling that she met his eyes a second time as if to be sure she had not been mistaken, and then settled back into her seat, somehow comforted, assured—as if he had spoken to her and told her not to fear. It was really as if something had looked out of their two souls and acknowledged a sort of mute introduction. And yet he had not been obtrusive, and almost immediately his eyes had been withdrawn from her face as if he would not intrude. He was looking now at the dreadful old man, rebuking him for his interest in her it would seem, rebuking most effectively yet without a word, for the old man wriggled around uneasily in his seat and turned his eyes away to look out of the window, the hate in his face getting the uppermost as he cast a furtive, fearsome glance at the younger man and then turned back to the window.

They were a curious pair; the younger man had the air of being the keeper of the older one. The girl wondered how they came to be traveling together, they seemed so absolutely alien to each other. It was obvious that the young man had some power over the other, and this fact gave the girl comfort.

To these two men the entrance of the lovely girl into the monotony of the journey was a refreshment. Even the old man, Scathlin, whose low type of life received only fleshly impressions, and who had grown up from his tainted babyhood without honor for any woman, felt the fineness of her nature, the rareness of her modest beauty as she came near.

To Jasper Holt she was the sudden startling revelation of some pure dream of his childhood, the reality of which he had come to doubt. His knowledge of the world told him that probably she was frail and human and selfish like all the rest if one came to know her, but for the sake of what she seemed to be he was glad of the vision, and would protect her at all costs because she was a woman and ought to have been perfect. That was his attitude toward the world of women at that time.

Nevertheless as he looked again at the pure profile turned now toward her window, and studied the sweet outline of the firm little chin, pleasant lips, the gentle contour of cheeks and lash and brow, the luminous eyes that were glowing for the moment at the stain of sunset beginning to trickle through the gloomy gray of the sky, he could not but feel that here was something different. It was something for which he had been hoping all his life—searching for, but never finding. Something it was good just to know existed;

something whose existence would make even a stranger better and braver and purer.

She was slight, small, exquisitely fashioned; dressed in some simple, clinging, dark blue material of form so suitable as to make one fail to notice just what it was. Sheer, white, rolled-back collar and cuffs set off the white throat and the small gloved hands; the close, dark blue hat with its graceful tilt and simple garnishing seemed just the loveliest setting for the beautiful face framed in its soft dark hair. Her face was wonderfully pure, free from self-consciousness and pride; yet she looked as if she knew her own mind and could stand like a rock for a principle. There was also a determined little uplift to her chin that showed a spirit of her own, and a fleeting dimple that promised a merry appreciation of humor if one knew her well enough; but the whole dainty person was good to look upon and Holt kept the vision within his consciousness while he covered Scathlin with his gaze.

He loathed his task of watching Scathlin, and somehow the sight of the pure-faced girl had made it even more distasteful. For almost two weeks now he had been at it, day and night. He had not let Scathlin out of his sight for one moment since he had found him in Pittsburgh two days after the theft of his wallet containing valuable papers, land grants, water rights and other documents relating to his silver mines and other property.

Holt had suspected the old man at once when the wallet was missing, partly because Scathlin had been seen twice in conversation with the man Harrington who was Holt's sworn enemy and who was doing all he could to ruin his prospects and dispute his rights to the water power which made the working of his mines possible; and partly because Scathlin had been dismissed summarily from Holt's employ but a few days previous to the disappearance of the property.

He had trailed Scathlin to Pittsburgh where he found him

mounted on a high stool in the station restaurant eating a comfortable breakfast. The old rascal turned white under his tan and stubble, and dropped his knife and fork loudly on the marble of the counter at the appearance of his former employer; but the cunning in his face had come at once to the front, and he welcomed Holt as if it were the pleasantest thing in the world to have him appear just at that lonely moment and eat breakfast with him.

It was Holt's way not to settle the matter right then and there by turning the old man over to the police on suspicion, but to attach himself to Scathlin and find out exactly where those papers were, and who were the man's employers in the theft. He was wary enough to know that Scathlin might have already got rid of the wallet, and he wished if possible to find out what he had done with the papers and get Scathlin into his power until he could make him produce them or tell their whereabouts.

Harrington was superintendent of large mine interests in Hawk Valley, located near Holt's veins of silver, and owned by an eastern syndicate. Holt knew that capital and cunning might do a great deal to cripple his interests if they once got him in their power. Therefore he had shadowed Scathlin day and night all these days. On pretense of wanting company for a pleasure trip he had gone wherever Scathlin professed to be going, giving him no opportunity to even telegraph to any of the other conspirators for money or instructions; eating with him, sleeping with him—at least pretending to sleep—sticking to him every minute and watching him every waking second.

It had not been a pleasant task. Scathlin was a foul-mouthed, foul-souled companion for any man to tie to, and his personal habits were anything but attractive. Time and again Holt had almost turned from his task with disgust, resolved to let his rights and all go rather than be tied to the creature another hour. Yet he had stuck to him; and now, after these many days of cunning and craftiness, of trickeries too numerous to mention, of attempted escape on Scathlin's part; after taking side trips to funerals of Scathlin's relatives who never had existed, except in imagination; visits to businessmen who were supposed to be hounding Scathlin to his death and yet who were never found; after all this they were on their way back to Hawk Valley! Scathlin had come to the end of his money and his wits, and had been compelled to accept the escort and financial aid of Holt back to the place from which he had started, because he did not dare to do anything else. This he did both on his own account and for the sake of his employers, who would not hesitate to leave him in the lurch to save themselves, and who had warned him above all things not to let Holt suspect his mission with those papers to the eastern syndicate. Besides, there was always the hope that he might yet escape and make his way back in time to present those papers to the man whom Harrington had said would pay him a big reward for bringing them. Harrington and his men could not have done it without suspicion, but the plan was that Scathlin should profess to have found something valuable to the syndicate and be willing to sell it at a good price.

It was no wonder that Scathlin's eyes had a hunted look, and his bad old face under its stubbly growth was almost pitifully desperate as he looked at the fresh face of the sweet young girl, and for the moment forgot his misery, gloating over her beauty, while Holt seemed to be engaged with the sunset view. But Holt caught the gleam in his victim's eye and his heart burned hotly within him. He could have crushed the creature then and there for the insolence of his gaze. He could have crushed him like vermin and felt no sin. All the man in him roused to resent the evil look.

"Scathlin!" His tone was cutting with command and the old man turned cringing and met the steely glance of his captor. Impatient and trembling with anger he began to look again out of the window as the crimson wrath surged up his leathery neck and suffused his coarse features.

The girl, half aware of what had been going on, turned and took it all in, a frightened color flickering up into her cheeks. Her eyes, growing large with vague horror, met Holt's steely gaze, saw it change and soften reassuringly, as if he were holding at bay a loathsome bloodhound and wished her to understand she need not fear. The girl, with one fleeting look of gratitude toward the young man, turned again to her window as if nothing had happened. In fact no onlooker would have suspected that anything at all had happened, and yet really a little drama had been enacted and all the actors understood it as thoroughly as if it had been spoken. But one word only had been audible, and the girl wasn't sure she had heard that aright.

The dusk dropped down and the train sped on over the plains.

And now the sunset stains grew deeper and blended into gold and crimson and lifted the gray into clear opal spaces of luminous beauty, spreading the panoply of color far along the horizon of the plain. It was a thing to make one look in awe, to hush evil thoughts and bring a holiness to hearts. Something of its calm and strength crept into the girl's expression as she watched it, and once she half turned to see if Holt were watching too. But Holt was facing the other way and could see only the fading trails of glory in the sky as it sped away from his gaze, though he had caught the reflection of wonder from her face, and averted his own eyes as if from too holy a sight. Those who knew Holt, or thought they knew him, would have laughed loud and long at such an idea of him, but it was true. The girl felt it as she turned safely back to her sunset.

Scathlin was not enjoying the view. He was looking furtively on every side to see if there could be by any chance a good place where he might risk throwing out that cursed wallet and hope to find it again. If only there were a station: he could risk dropping it out of the window near some water tank or something. But the plain slid by, a level monotony,

broken only by the rose and emerald and gold of the setting
sun. Scathlin grew more and more desperate. It was growing
dark, and he dared not throw the wallet where he could not
find it again, or where someone else might find it. Yet they
were nearing Hawk Valley. The morning would bring them
within the ranging of Holt's men—that brand of trained and
devoted outlaws who were as relentless in their justice as
they were careless of their lives. No mercy was to be expected from their hands if once he fell among them. He shivered as a tall shaft of a bare tree, dead and stark, stood out in
the distance against the clear gold of the sunset line. It was
on such a tree he had seen a cattle thief hang ghastly against
the sky, as he rode by once just at nightfall. It might easily
be his fate before another sunset. If he could not get away in
the night all chance of escape before they reached Hawk
Valley was gone, for well he knew Jasper Holt's men were
set at intervals along the way, sentinels ready to head him
off. And what treatment could he expect from either Jasper
Holt or his men with that incriminating wallet in his pocket?
He had been a fool to take up with Harrington's offer.
Money or no money, it wasn't worth the risk. He was getting
to be an old man and not so ready to face death as when his
blood was hot and his hand steady. He had not even any
weapons of defense, thanks to his grim captor who had dis-
armed him while he slept, the first night of their journey together. There had never been any open recognition of the
fact between them, save that one glance as Scathlin put his
hand to the pocket where it had been and was not. He had
charged with his eyes in one look of helpless fury, and Holt's
clear gray eyes had met his unflinchingly in acknowledg-
ment. That had been all, but Scathlin knew then that there
was nothing for him but to evade Holt and get away if possible. He would stand no chance in an open conflict, and his
captor was untiringly vigilant. He glanced again at the stern
face opposite him, wondering what would be the fate to
which he was surely, swiftly hastening. State prison? Or

would they take the law into their own hands? He knew what that might mean only too well, and again the desperate look passed over his face with hate and murder looking dimly from his eyes. How he would like to spring at that slim brown throat opposite him and throttle the life from the young fellow. Only a kid—a mere kid—and yet he had withstood many, and had power to crush Scathlin in spite of all his boasted cunning. The look of a serpent crept into the little gleaming eyes of the old man as he noticed the quick glance his companion cast at the girl across the aisle; and his own eyes followed, filled with hate. Yes, he would like to drive his fat, hairy fingers into the white throat of the girl before the eyes of her gallant defender. If only he had Holt helpless! But instead, here he was, helpless himself! And he must find a way to escape before morning, or else get rid of that wallet in some safe way. Surely, surely Holt would be off his guard sometimes for a little space. He had scarcely slept a wink for four days; how could he endure it much longer?

But Scathlin's cogitations were cut short by the entrance of the conductor at last and he turned to watch the girl as she spoke to him.

"I was to have had a section reserved for me," she was saying to the conductor. "My brother-in-law, Mr. James Harrington of Hawk Valley, arranged for it, and telegraphed me that it was all right. See, I have the telegram. But the porter said I must come in here until I saw you because I had no ticket for the pullman."

She held out the yellow envelope and the conductor looked at it.

"Your brother-in-law's name is Harrington? You are going to Hawk Valley?"

He looked at her sharply. "Well, just wait a few minutes till I go through the next car and then I'll see to it. It ought to be all right."

He bustled on his way, attending to his passengers, and the girl sat back again to wait.

At the name "Harrington" Scathlin had turned with a start and looked toward the girl; but even in the act he caught the narrow gleam of Holt's half-closed eyes, and, remembering, turned back again to his window while his thoughts went pounding into new channels. He had made a mistake, of course, to let Holt see that he had heard, so he kept his eyes toward the window until it grew quite dark. But he had a plan at last. In another minute he got upon his feet, yawning, and declared his intention of getting a drink of water from the cooler at the other end of the car.

"Good idea!" said Holt, rising and following his captive down the aisle lazily.

Scathlin reached the cooler first and took his drink, while Holt stood waiting for the cup and let Scathlin go back to his seat alone, apparently not noticing him. Scathlin settled back in his seat with one eye on Holt, and one eye on the girl.

Holt stood drinking in a leisurely way, apparently interested in looking through the glass of the door into the next car though he was fully aware that Scathlin was fumbling in the inner pocket of his flannel shirt. He lingered, hoping that the old man would do something which would make him more certain of what he already believed to be true, and saw Scathlin finally, after repeated fumbling under the shirt, draw forth a small dark object that, in the one swift glimpse Holt had of it, looked like his own leather wallet in search of which he had come this long hard journey. Anxious to see what Scathlin's next move was to be, he remained quietly standing and still apparently looking through the car door, though not a move of Scathlin's was lost upon him. To his amazement he suddenly saw Scathlin bend forward and pick up something from the car floor, then lean toward the girl in the opposite seat and put the object in her lap, at the same time speaking to her. Had the man picked up some-

thing the girl had dropped or was he. . . ? Preposterous! The
fellow wouldn't dare, with a strange girl. She was smiling
and looking down at the thing in her lap and seemed to be
thanking him. She had probably dropped her handkerchief
or pocketbook and Scathlin had picked it up. Holt sauntered
leisurely back to his seat and found Scathlin fumbling with
his shoelace. He studied him narrowly and fancied that he
detected a look of cunning satisfaction on the stubbly old
face, yet was puzzled to know what caused it. Had the
scoundrel dared to give those papers to the girl when he
stood in full view? It seemed incredible . . . and yet? If he
had, Holt's hands were pretty well tied and he had two to
watch instead of one. He didn't like the idea of shadowing
this beautiful young woman.

Just then the conductor returned and spoke to the girl.

"Miss Grayson, your berth's reserved for you all right, but
it was in the name of Harrington. It's section seven in the
next car. This your baggage? Come this way and I'll show
you."

The girl followed the conductor, with a half-hesitating
glance toward Scathlin who was engaged with his shoe. Holt
noticed she held her handbag clasped tightly as if she were
afraid it might be taken from her. When she was gone the
night settled down unpleasantly about them and Scathlin,
apparently worn out, snored as he had not dared to do for a
week. But Holt sat up and studied his problem. He could not
afford to take any chances on sleep that night; moreover his
heart was in a tumult. This girl was coming to Hawk Valley,
to visit the Harringtons. She was a sister of Mrs. Harrington,
the handsomest woman, the best dressed woman, the most
influential woman in all that Valley. Would he ever see the
girl? Sometimes, from afar perhaps . . . and a bitter look
swept over his face.

Scathlin slept on, with his coarse lower jaw down
dropped, and all his unpleasant features relaxed. He was no
charming picture to look upon. Holt noticed that there was

no longer that furtive grasp of one hand upon his breast which had been since their journey together had begun. Scathlin's calloused hands, with their grasping look of cunning, were lying idly by his side, and Scathlin himself was enjoying a well-earned rest, his heavily shod feet sprawled out under Holt's seat.

The night droned on; the train sped on its way through the darkness, and still Holt sat wide awake and thinking.

"I can't quite figure things out," he said to himself as he settled back in a new position.

Chapter 2

Meanwhile Jean Grayson had followed her bustling conductor into the sleeper with a sense of deep relief. She had been frankly frightened since the rough old tramp-looking creature across the aisle had landed a worn-looking wallet surreptitiously in her lap and asked if he hadn't heard her say she was going to Mr. Harrington at Hawk Valley, and would she be so good as to give that case of important papers to him and not let anyone else know she had it?

She had accepted the trust because she did not know what else to do; and after all, it seemed a simple enough request. The man explained that he had to go off in another direction at the next stop and could not deliver the goods himself and it was most important that it get to her brother-in-law at once. There did not seem to be any good reason why she should refuse, and yet it had frightened her, and she wished with all her heart that she had gone with the conductor to see about the sleeper and not stayed here to have this dirty old leather case put into her keeping by that dirty old man. She did not know what to do with it. She hated to put it in her dear little new handbag, and she restrained her well cut nose from a shrinking sniff as she hastily put it out of sight.

She had sat looking out of the darkened window with her heart in a tumult as the tall young man with the fine eyes and the air of reckless assurance came back to his seat. What had he to do with the old fellow? Could he be his son? No, never! But did he know about the important papers? Could he have put the old man up to giving them to her, so that, under some pretense or other, he himself might speak to her? She did not dare to look his way lest he should presume upon the old man's speaking. This, her first western trip, was a fearsome thing to her, although she reveled in the joy of it.

Yet, when she rose to follow the conductor and gave one swift comprehensive glance toward the opposite seat, she saw a respectful pair of gray eyes looking interestedly at her, with nothing presumptuous in them, and she instantly felt that there was no need to fear that young man. He might be dressed like a cowboy, but he had eyes like a gentleman.

Miss Grayson was tired, for she had come a long journey, stopping a day on the way with relatives who had taken her sightseeing and kept her going every minute, so that she was glad to creep into her berth as soon as the porter had made it up.

She shrank in dislike from the leather case in her handbag, and after some hesitation took it out and wrapped it in a page from a magazine she had brought with her. She could not bear to have the thing touch all her nice fresh handkerchiefs and dainty little articles. It seemed contaminating. She had a half impulse to throw it away or lose it; and then her conscience reproached her loudly for so dishonorable a thought. The papers might be valuable, of course, and in that case her brother-in-law would have just cause to blame her if she did not bring them. At the same time she hated the thought of carrying around anything that had been in the possession of that repulsive-looking man.

As she settled herself to sleep and drew around her the folds of the soft silk pullman robe that had been her mother's parting surprise, loving thoughts of those she had left behind her filled her mind. All the little tender words, looks and acts of loving sacrifice that she might be well fitted out for this journey, came flocking to be recognized, until unbidden tears filled her eyes. This silken robe was an extravagance, she knew, and would be paid for by many a denial on the part of father and mother, but it represented their great love for her. A thought of what they would have felt about her being accosted by that rough man and asked to carry that package for him came to trouble her, yet what other possible thing was there for her to do but to accept it? It certainly could not be dynamite or an infernal machine. Her mother would have thought of something of that nature the first thing.

Her father? Yes, her father would undoubtedly have approved of her taking the package. Her father was one who never thought of himself when anything in the shape of duty demanded attention, and he had brought her up with the same feeling. Anyway, now that she had taken it and agreed to deliver it, there seemed nothing more to be done but to keep her word, and it was a simple enough affair, of course, and after all, quite reasonable. Why should it bother her so?

Nevertheless, it mingled with her dreaming thoughts as she drifted off to sleep, and a kind of assurance with regard to it came as she remembered the steady, clear eyes of the younger man.

Softly in her silken wrapping she lay and slept while the monotonous hum of the rushing train only lulled her to deeper slumber.

Suddenly, in the midst of the commonplace sounds of the journey there came a grinding, grating shriek as of strong metal hard pressed and unable to withstand. A crash, a jolt, then terrible confusion. The very foundations of the earth seemed upshaken, the cars climbing through the awful air, then pitching, writhing, tossing, and at last settling uncertainly in strange positions, while the night was filled with horrid sounds too varying to analyze. Cries of women and children; groans of men in mortal agony; breaking glass and splintering timbers; rending of metal in reluctant, discordant clang! And below, rising menacingly to threaten all, came the lurid glare of flame, the wild, exultant crackle of fire that knows its opportunity and power; the desperate hysterical clamor of those who have discovered it, and the mad, brave shouts of those who would attempt to conquer it.

Jean Grayson awoke in dazed bewilderment. For a moment the noise seemed a part of her dream; her strange, huddled position on the wood at the foot of her berth, a figment of her imagination. But almost at once the cold breath from the broken window brought her to her senses. An accident! It had come then! The thing which her mother had feared and tried to provide against. She was in a railroad accident all alone and out in the wilds of the west where she was utterly unacquainted with anyone! It was characteristic of Jean that, when she realized her plight, she thought first of how her mother would take the news, and not of how *she* would bear the experience, or whether it meant life and death to herself. That she must get out of danger and let her mother know of her safety was her instant impulse, and from that moment her senses were keenly on the alert for every detail.

Her mother's horrors of railroad accidents made the possibilities of her present position as plain to her as if she had lived the whole experience before. She seemed to comprehend in a flash just what had happened, and about the position the car was in at the time. The lurid glare that was already leaping and flickering outside showed jagged glass in the window frame, and scattered gleaming fragments all about her. She must move carefully not to be cut by them. Fire! That was the next thing she took in. That meant that her only hope of life was to get out at once. Cautiously she looked out of the window to get a better idea of things and her heart stood still with the horror of it all. For one little terrible second she forgot her mother's fears and felt her own gasping, choking terror at what was before her. One moment she faced a probable death, felt her helplessness, and gave a cry of anguish for those who had always protected her from peril, and who were far away. Then her own brave courage rose and steadied her nerves. She resolved not to die if there were any possible way out of it; and terror relaxed its hold upon her at sight of her courage.

With resolute determination she held her horror-stricken eyes to take in the situation in detail. She must know everything, see everything, if she were to save herself, for she comprehended readily enough that as things were it was everyone for himself. No one was going to risk his life to hunt her up and drag her forth from the pile of doomed cars.

The train had been crossing a river when the crash came. There was water down below, black and terrifying in the glare of flame that was leaping like great tongues among the ruins just ahead. She could not tell if the cause of the accident had been a broken bridge or a collision, and knew little about such things to judge. The cars were piled one upon another in wild confusion, and the pullman in which she was immured was standing on its forward end almost perpendicularly. The engine was overturned and fire was creeping upward and threatening the whole mass; while below, the great black stretch of water reflected the sight, making doubly terrible every feature.

Jean drew back and attempted to look out into the car, but the curtains were jammed tight by some heavy object which had fallen against them, and she could get no idea of the situation on that side. When she at last succeeded in pulling the curtain away enough to look she saw only a dark precipice below, with writhing forms and jumbled shapes. No one seemed to have thought of any way of escape for the passengers, or to be making any attempt to get them out before it was too late. The shouts and cries that came from below had no authority among them. It was plain that the only hope of escape was through the broken window and down into that abyss of water and fire below.

Jean drew back and felt carefully around for her shoes. She could not take much with her, and she must work rapidly. The shoes and little handbag were almost under her, and she drew on the shoes, fastening a button or two. She hesitated a second with her hand on the precious bag. All her money, her trunk check and her little bits of jewelry were in it. She must save them if she could. Those papers that had been trusted to her were there also. Quickly she stuffed the bag within the breast of her garments and fastened it there with a large safety pin, with which she had fastened the berth curtain the night before, when a refractory button kept coming undone. Her heart gave a leap of excitement. Now, in her need, she remembered it, and groping, found it there in the semi-darkness, big enough to be found when wanted, and to hold the bag in safety.

She gave one frightened look out the window at the growing, widening horrors below, and then began slowly, cautiously to creep through, feet first. It was a dangerous painful task, as there was much glass still adhering firmly to the window frame, and she found that she had to draw back at first and hunt up her hair brush with which to break away the sharp edges and make the opening large enough.

It seemed an hour, though in reality it was but a moment or two, before she finally succeeded in getting out of the window, so that she clung, suspended, both arms still inside the berth, but her body hanging over the abyss of black depths mingled with flames.

Dark shapes were moving about down there; dark, moaning creatures were dropping with sickening splashes into the water. She dared not look to see if they rose. Her head grew light, and she felt her fingers slipping. Her strength would not hold her long, and she was almost on the point of trying to creep back inside the berth when a long cry as of the lost, mingled with moans and screams of women and children, arose from below, and she saw a great sheet of fire leap up and lick the lower end of the very car to which she clung. She could feel the heat of it where she was, and but for the slight inclination of the car it would have been between her and the water.

With a low moan of horror, she closed her eyes and let herself drop. Down, down, she felt herself falling, through eons of time and space, and knew that she was wondering how her mother would bear it when she heard. Then the shock of the water, and darkness closed over her in a smothering chill.

Chapter 3

She came up again gasping and choking, aware of the shouts and the noise, of the struggling figures and dropping objects; aware that she was only one more in the way and might better have stayed where she was; then struck out feebly; but something fell upon her head, something soft like a pillow perhaps, but enough to put her under water again, and she felt that this was the end.

When she could get her breath again a strong arm was pulling her away from the crowd and noise. There were things in the way, people and heavy objects, but she was being steered through them all, out of the labyrinth of horror and into dark, still waters.

There followed a long stretch of toiling through the water, which seemed like ages, when her breath came in gasps, and her heart seemed pounding her very life away as she ploughed through the blackness, making a brave effort to keep up with the strong, steady strokes beside her, though scarcely aware of what she was doing. Life seemed going from her ebb by ebb and it was not worthwhile to try to hold on to it any longer, and yet the memory of her mother's fears kept her trying. After that she kept on, unconscious of anything save that she must keep going, she must, she *must*. Finally even that dim impulse flickered out and the water flowed about her very soul; softly, dreamily, possessingly. Yet still she was drawn on and on through the blackness to a distant shore.

He dragged her up on the bank at last, the man who had saved her out of the chaos of peril and brought her with him at the expense of his own almost exhausted strength. He was gasping and all but finished himself when he dropped beside her among the tall reeds that served to shelter them from the night, and for a few moments they lay quiet, passive; the girl unconscious, the man panting for breath and unable as yet to think what to do next; two stranger souls in common peril, knowing naught of each other or of what was before them.

In a moment, however, the chill of the night roused the man, and he shivered and sat up. Whoever it was that he had saved—a woman—her long hair and trammeling garments had already told him that—she would die if she lay long in that condition. What could he do?

He shivered again and got up. He shook the water from himself. His splendid strength reasserted itself, and his breath was steady now. He was surprised that even a swim like that, encumbered as he was with heavy clothing and shoes, and bearing another helpless creature, should have knocked him out so completely. Then he reflected that he had lost much sleep during the past few days; still, that was not enough to make him feel so worthless. He shook himself again and stretched his muscles, as he used to do on the football field in his boyhood days, after a knockout, when he heard the call back into the game. If ever there was a call to come back into the game it was now, for this woman would die if he did not do something at once.

The night was wild and chill. Across the river, farther away than he dreamed they had come, the sky was lurid with the fire that flared grotesquely against the darkness. The current must have carried them downstream as they crossed. He had thought to go back and help save others so soon as he had this one safe, but the way was far and this woman was apparently helpless, perhaps unconscious, or at least exhausted. If she lay here in her wet garments she would die from the cold. He must get her to her feet and keep her warm somehow.

Stooping, he lifted her light weight and bore her farther up the bank into the woods, then laid her down on the ground and knelt to listen to her heart. It was beating weakly. If only he had fire or stimulant or both! Perhaps there was a house somewhere near. He would carry her a little way and see. So he picked her up again, holding her close to keep her warm, and struggled on through the thick undergrowth in the darkness.

That night was an experience to be remembered through a lifetime. The young strength of the man seemed to revive with the necessity, and he carried the woman a long distance before, with the warmth of his body and the motion of the going, the girl came to her senses and was able to walk for herself.

For the first instant of her waking to consciousness her soul seemed to stand still with horror. Where was she and who was carrying her? What would happen to her? Would she ever see her home and friends again? The questions rushed madly through her mind and almost paralyzed her thoughts for an instant. Then memory reasserted itself. All the facts of the disaster as she had seen them, came back. She knew that whoever was carrying her must have saved her out of kindness. She knew that he must have had to swim alone during at least a part of the way through the water, for she could distinctly remember, now, the horror of being unable to keep up any longer. Then there was something else, a kindly, strong, impersonal clasp that made her unafraid. After a minute she signified her ability to walk, and he set her down at once, yet held her arm and put his own about her for support.

"If you can walk it will keep you warm," he said briefly; and with no apology for his arm about her he hurried her on. It was all she could do to keep up with his pace, and when her feet faltered he seemed to almost lift her from the ground as he still strode on.

"We must keep going," he said again, as if he had no more breath to waste in words. On and on they went, but still they did not come to any human habitation. Finally, when he saw that she could go no further, and that she needed rest, he made her sit down in a sheltered place behind some trees. Later, when she was almost asleep, she knew her head was resting against his shoulder. Once in the night she awoke and saw a fire blazing near her, and realized that a man's coat was spread over her and she was warm and comparatively dry. There was no one in sight, but she heard a step not far away and the crackling of breaking branches. She did not wonder how the fire came. She slept again.

It was in the early dawn that she awoke sharply as if she had been called, and stretching her stiff limbs looked wildly about her, startlingly aware of the night that had passed and her strange isolation with an unknown man.

He lay upon the ground at the other side of the fire which had been piled high with wood and was burning beautifully, his strong fine figure stretched wearily at full length, the brown curly hair tumbled back from his bronzed face, which in spite of its soil and grime showed a manly beauty. The utter weariness and relaxation of his body made him seem like a boy.

The girl looked and wondered, and turned away to remember. He must have had to swim with her quite a distance, and drag her to land after she ceased to help herself. Also he must have carried her a long way. He had held her when she walked beside him, and had sat against a tree and made her lean against him part of the time while she slept. Then how did he get that fire? Some mystery known to woodcraft no doubt. She glanced at herself with the thick brown coat tucked carefully about her still. She touched it softly, almost reverently with her fingertips. It was dry! He had contrived to dry it and put it about her!

She looked over at the man again. He wore a brown flannel shirt and heavy trousers like the coat. He must have been cold himself without his coat while she slept in comfort. And he had stayed awake all night to keep the fire going to dry her things and keep her warm!

There were tears in her eyes as her glance lingered on the boyish face. She pictured writing to her mother what he was like, this strong man like an angel who had saved her. Then she shuddered at the thought of the wreck and all she had gone through. What would have been her fate if he had not put his arm beneath her when she was sinking?

Presently, as the sun crept higher up the sky and lit the world with rose and golden light, she stole shyly from her couch under the tree and, stepping softly, came to where he was and tucked the coat carefully about him, as he lay, one cheek pillowed on his arm. Her hand brushed lightly against his hair, and she marveled at its softness—like a baby's. His skin, too, had that clear ruddy glow of perfect health, even beneath the grime of the night. She looked down on him with wonder and a great gratitude that seemed to almost overwhelm her. Perhaps all people felt so toward men who had saved their lives; but Jean Grayson had never before seen a man who seemed one-half so strong and great and good as this mere boy looked to her now in the early light of morning, asleep upon the ground and soundly unaware of her tender ministration.

She slipped away quietly without wakening him, and stood a moment looking about her upon the strange unknown world, wondering where she was. What state was this? She could not even be sure of that. Then she looked down at herself.

She wore the long black pullman robe of soft silk, sadly draggled now and torn in two or three places. How beautiful and fine it had been but a few short hours before! And her other pretty clothes that had been bought and made so carefully at the cost of such family sacrifice. Were they all gone? Would her trunk burn up? Or had it gone on ahead of her when she had stopped to visit her friends and so escaped destruction? But she dismissed the thought as unworthy of one who had but just escaped with her life. What were clothes beside life? But how was she to go on with her journey looking like this? Her pretty traveling gown! She felt a pang for that. Well, she must do the best she could.

Her hair was the worst of all, but she could put that right. Her precious handbag! She put her hand to her breast to be sure it was there safe. Yes, it was still fastened to her clothing, though the pin had torn away and there was but a small hold of the cloth still in it. She pulled it out and examined it, seated behind a tree away from the fire and the sleeping man. Yes, the bag was safe, and its contents, but its beauty was gone, for the thin leather finish was blistered and peeling from the inner lining. The things inside were all there, even the strange man's leather case, wrapped in a wet pulp of paper. She took the paper off and threw it from her; then realizing how few worldly goods she was now possessed of, she reached and spread the paper out to dry. It would be needed, of course.

Her small store of money was safe, and her bits of pins and watch, the little timepiece ticking bravely on as if it were alive and trying to be cheerful under adverse circumstances.

Jean took out her combs and hairpins which she had stowed in the pocket of her handbag that they might be easily found in the morning, and felt rich indeed to have them. They would assist very materially in her toilet.

With the aid of the combs she presently had her hair soft and shining in its accustomed coils and fluffy masses, for fortunately for her appearance that morning, her hair was of the kind that tries to curl in spite of floods and winds, and it fluffed its prettiest with the first rays of the sun glinting over it.

The handbag held, among other things, a needle and both black and white thread. With their aid Jean mended the rents in her robe, and managed to make herself look quite presentable. Then wrapping the damp paper again about the displeasing leather case she bestowed it with a shrug of dislike into the disfigured bag once more and started forth in search of water to wash off the stains of the night.

Her hands were badly scratched and one had been bleeding. She remembered the glass and wondered now how she had escaped with as few scratches as she had.

But water she could not find within sight of the fire and she dared not go further lest she get lost. She found, however, a dense growth of bushes bearing great luscious berries, and though they were not exactly like any berries with which she was familiar she decided that they were probably edible, and gathered her hands full. Then, coming softly back near the fire, she looked around for a suitable place for the breakfast table. The sleeper had not awakened. She went about cautiously and found a great flat rock quite near where he lay that would do beautifully. Here she laid her berries on a dish of green leaves, with their points all radiating from the center and two large leaves, one on each side, for plates.

Then remembering something, she opened her handbag again.

The day before, when her cousins had taken her sightseeing, they had treated her to an ice cream soda, with which had been served a tiny envelope of wax paper containing three small wafer crackers. She had put hers in the bag, laughingly declaring that she would eat them on the train when she was hungry, and one cousin had added her envelope as well. She had not thought of them when she opened it before, but now she hurried to bring them forth. Of course they would be spoiled! But no—the envelopes were still about them, and though somewhat damp they had retained their shape and looked exceedingly good to a hungry mortal.

Eagerly she set them forth, three on each leaf-plate, and hurried back to the bush to get more berries.

Either the soft stepping feet as they went lightly through the grass, or the falling of a stick into the ashes of the fire disturbed the sleeper, for he awoke suddenly and looked about him.

The girl was gone! That was his first thought.

The look of boyishness fell away from him in a flash, and he rose to his feet and gazed about him anxiously, alertly, as if he feared danger near. Then his eyes fell on the flat rock with its mimic banquet spread forth! A flood of wonder and delight swept into his face and a great tenderness, such as no one of his friends or foes ever dreamed would be hid away anywhere in his nature. He had never played dolls on a rock with some little girl, and moss and acorns for carpet and dishes, but the "playhouse" spirit was there in his heart and leapt at once into consciousness. A table for two! The woman had provided a meal even in the wilderness!

He had been turning about in his mind how he was to get something to eat with neither powder nor hook, and here she had been quicker than he and breakfast was all prepared!

Something stirred in Jasper Holt's heart that he had not known was there, a longing for companionship in his life and home; the table set for two and someone to care! He had never felt its need before and he did not call it by that name now. He merely experienced a strangely beautiful thrill at the new possibilities that life suddenly revealed to him; something higher and better and infinitely sweeter than any of the ambitions and ideals he had hitherto entertained.

He was still standing, gazing in wonder at the table, when the quick crackling of a twig made known her return.

Chapter 4

She stood for an instant, framed in the opening of the trees, her eyes bright, her lips parted, her cheeks pink with the exertion of picking the berries. Both her hands were full of the fruit.

"Oh, good morning!" she said shyly before he could think what to say. "I hope I didn't waken you. I am sure you needed to sleep longer."

His eyes glowed with admiration, and he stood startled at her beauty, marveling that she had accomplished a toilet with so little at her command.

"How about you?" he said, watching her with admiring glance, "You didn't need any sleep at all, I suppose. You were just about all in last night and no mistake."

"Yes, I guess I was," she answered penitently, "and I'm afraid I gave you a lot of trouble, not being able to walk when I should. I can never thank you enough! You saved my life, of course! I never should have got to shore. . . ."

"Forget it!" he said with a smile, "it was nothing."

"And you had to carry me a long distance, I am sure you did. I can remember a long time when I know I was not walking. You must be worn out!"

"Why, you're not heavy," he said amusedly, eyeing her slender frame. "I could carry you a good deal farther than that and not play out. I'm glad to see you look so rested this morning. I didn't expect it after what you went through. I see you have your nerve with you. It was a pretty nervy thing you did, you know, that stunt of dropping out of the window. I had just got out myself further down and climbed on shore to see if there was anything I could do for anyone, when I saw you drop, and I thought you were gone for sure.

There were rocks and timbers all around there and heavy things falling, and I thought I saw your finish."

"And so you came and rescued me!" she said, with a look of gratitude that brought a flush over his strong, tanned face.

"Oh, I just floated over that way to see if I could pick up anybody. I couldn't tell who I was fishing out when I took hold of you, there were so many sounds and things around."

"Well, I . . . I can't thank you enough now," she said, and there was a glisten of tears in her eyes. "I know it was wonderful what you did."

"Oh, forget it!" he said again, laughing lightly. "It was bad enough all around, and we were lucky to get off as we did. But we aren't out of the woods yet. We'd better let bygones be bygones for the present anyway. Don't you want to sit down?"

Jean smilingly acquiesced, dropping down beside the rock with her berries, and leaning over to arrange them with the rest.

"These ought to be washed," she said as she arranged them on the leaf-plate in the center, "but I couldn't find any water."

"Water won't be so hard to find, but we haven't anything to put it in," he answered laughing, "and besides, we oughtn't to mind a little dirt after all we've been through. I doubt if the berries I usually get are washed anyway. But if I had anything to carry it in, I'd find some water. I haven't even a hat. . . ."

"Why, I had a little drinking cup, but I don't remember whether it's in my bag or not. Perhaps I put it in the suitcase, though I think I left it in my bag."

She laid down the last berries, and wiping the stains from her fingers on the grass she opened the bag which she had slipped through the belt of her robe and made to hang at her side. It was rather full and when it was opened the leather wallet, wrapped in its damp paper, fell out on the ground, and the paper came unfolded, revealing what it contained.

The young man stooped gravely, a dark flush rising to his cheeks, and picked it up. He did not look startled nor surprised and she noticed nothing strange in his manner as he handed it to her. Afterward she wondered at that.

The cup did not materialize, but there were the two little wax paper envelopes, which might hold water. She held them out to him, and looking up, their eyes met.

"Why, you are the man who sat opposite to me in the day coach," she said in pleased surprise, "I didn't recognize you before without your hat on. But I remember thinking when I went to the other car that you had a face that one need not be afraid of. I was a little frightened by the old man who sat with you—he spoke to me—but when I saw you I was not afraid anymore. Mother says I'm always going by my intuitions, but I think this time you've proved them true. I knew you were a person to be trusted."

He looked at her wonderingly, a strange expression of wistfulness crossing his face.

"People don't often feel that way about me," he said in a strange low tone that seemed to hide a good deal more behind the words than was said. "I guess you're the first person who has trusted me in a long time."

"Oh," she said, looking at him seriously, "I guess you don't know ... or else...." She paused as if in doubt whether to finish the sentence.

"Or else what, please?" he asked with compelling gaze.

"I was going to say or else they don't know you; but that sounds rather bold for a stranger to say when I've only known you a few hours. But I've had opportunity to prove that what I thought about you was true. Perhaps it's that you do not always let people see the nice things in you the way you have had to let me because of my need."

"Well, that's a new way of painting my character, I must say. I rather like it myself but I doubt if anybody would recognize it for me. I wouldn't mind being that way, believe me, and I thank you for sizing me up in that style. I'll think it over, but I'm afraid you've got your characters mixed and I'm not in your line at all. However, I'm glad you think so. Now I'll see what I can do about water."

He took the two envelopes as if they had been cut glass goblets and walked away into the woods. In a few minutes he returned with them dripping, his own face ruddy with recent washing, and his curls still damp and dark above his forehead; while the strong hands that held the makeshift cups were clean as water could make them.

"Would you like to wash your face?" he asked as he held out the cup for her to drink. "Never mind the berries, they are all right as they are. I'll show you the water and then come back to guard the food. We don't know what wild creature may find our table and make off with our breakfast."

"Oh, would they do that?" laughed Jean, interested. "Wouldn't that be funny?"

"It might not be so funny if we don't strike a ranch pretty soon," said Holt, looking serious. "We need all that breakfast to help us on our way after the night we've spent."

"I will not wash my face until after breakfast," said Jean decidedly, coming back to the rock and seating herself by one of the leaf-plates. "Sit down, please, and break your fast for we are not running any risks on this trip. I want to get to a telegraph office and send word to my mother and father. They will hear about the accident and will be terribly frightened about me. You won't mind my eating with unwashed hands, will you?"

"I should worry!" declared Holt, seating himself on the other side of the rock with the ease of one who is as much at home on the ground as on a chair.

"These crackers are a little limp," said Jean, "but it was the best I could do considering that they were submerged for a long time."

"They're great," said Holt, sampling one, "but how did you happen to have them?"

She told him merrily of her visit the day before and how she had saved them.

"They're all you have!" said Holt suddenly, "you may need the rest of them before we are through. Put these away and keep them till you need them. I'll just eat the berries. I'm used to going without for a long time."

"Wasn't your life the only one you had when you risked it to save me?" asked Jean, looking at him earnestly. "I guess you'll get half of all there is or I won't have *any.*"

Holt looked at her admiringly.

"That's all right, but I'd rather you saved them. You're a woman."

"That may be all right, but I *won't,*" said Jean decidedly, "and I won't eat another bite until you eat yours."

He looked at her with the glow of appreciation growing in his eyes. He never had seen a girl like this.

"You're all right!" he said at last. "You're the real thing. You're a good fellow. I guess we're partners, then."

He held out his hand as he would have done to a man, and the girl, with a quick appreciation of his words, laid her small berry-stained hand in the big, hard one.

"Thank you," she said earnestly. "That rather puts us on equal footing, doesn't it? But I'm not so foolish as to think we really are. I know it's only a very little bit that I can do on this expedition. You do all the big, grand, hard things. But you mustn't deny me the chance to do the little things I *can* do; and sharing, or even going without sometimes, belongs to my part. I haven't forgotten yet that you saved my life."

He looked at the little hand wonderingly and held it gently in his own, with just a slight, lingering, wistful closing of his strong fingers around it; then let it go as though he were afraid he might crush it, it seemed to him so frail and exquisite and fine.

"I can tell you one thing," he said, "you're *some improvement* on the last partner I had." Jean gave him a swift, re-

lieved look. "That horrid old man?" she asked compre-
hendingly. He nodded, but searched her face keenly, as
if he would make sure of something. He seemed satisfied,
however, with the frank look in her clear eyes and said
no more. Perhaps he hoped she would confide in him—or
perhaps he liked her all the better that she did not—who
knows?

They ate their meager breakfast hungrily, yet lingered
over it happily. The morning seemed to each as an exquisite
treasure of time loaned to them for this once, and there fell a
charm upon them that neither quite understood; only they
were conscious of joy in being alive and having each other.
The experiences of the night and the unusual surroundings
did away with all conventionalities and feelings of embarrassment they would otherwise have had in their strange
plight; and their laughter mingled and rang out among the
trees joyously on that early beautiful morning after the
disaster.

He led her down to the stream to wash while he made a
basket of leaves, pinned together with stems, and filled it full
of berries.

"We may need them for dinner," he remarked as he went
back to the bushes.

Jean finished her ablutions, and, washing out her handkerchief, filled it also with berries; and thus provided with a
lunch, they started on their way.

After coming out of the woods they climbed first to the
highest point of ground near them and surveyed the landscape in every direction, but nothing more serene on a summer morning could be found anywhere than was before
them. Turn which way they would there was no sign of disaster or wreck. The soft, green hills on every side hid the
secret of its location, and the world lay spread before them
without a hint of ravage or distress. There was absolutely no
way to tell direction except in a general way of the sun;
and where the wreck had been it was impossible even to

speculate, for they could not tell how they had come in the darkness.

This gave a new aspect to their situation. Holt had been thinking during the night that if they could work their way back to the wreck they would probably reach home more quickly, for surely by this time a relief train must have come. But now he saw that it was useless to consider that longer. They must just press on till they came to a house, where possibly they could procure horses, and certainly information as to their whereabouts. There was a reason why he wished to get back to the world as quickly as possible; yet something taught him to be glad that necessity had given him this day or part of a day, whichever it was to be, with this girl.

He looked down almost tenderly at the bright, trusting face that smiled up at him so bravely. He had a sudden comprehending glimpse of what it must be to a girl, such as he could see she was, to be dropped down into a strange world, far from home and protection, in company with a man about whom she knew nothing.

"Tough luck," he said, answering the questions in her eyes, "but don't you worry, we'll get out sooner or later."

"I'm not worrying," she answered earnestly, "but I was wishing we knew how to send a telegram to my father. I wonder if someday they won't perfect the system so that people can send messages from anywhere without any instruments, if they just know how."

"That would be great," said Holt, thoughtfully. "I'd send one this minute to the nearest inhabited point for two good saddle horses. Can you ride?"

"A little. I've never had much opportunity. Father used to keep a horse, but when we moved to our present home he had to give it up. There wasn't really any need for it. But I'm to ride while I'm away visiting my sister." Her face brightened at the thought, and then clouded. "That is, if we ever get there. . . ."

"Oh, we'll get there all right," said Holt easily, taking his bearings and deciding which way to strike out. "You're Mrs. Harrington's sister, aren't you?"

"Why yes, how did you know?" said the girl with a ring of relief in her voice. "You know my sister, then?" This was almost equivalent to an introduction, and she knew her mother would be particular about that.

"I heard you tell the conductor," he said. "Shall we start? We've got a good journey to travel judging by the look of things. This way," and he led her down the slope out into the open where they could see where they were going.

"But you wouldn't have remembered all this time if you hadn't known who she was," she flashed back, smiling. "How pleased Eleanor will be when she knows one of her own friends took care of me and saved my life."

Holt's face darkened suddenly and he did not answer at once. When he did his voice was cold and hard like a sudden storm on a sunny day.

"I don't think she'd exactly call me her friend!"

His eyes were narrowed, and his chin was set with a haughty lift.

"Well, acquaintance, then," said Jean brightly. "Eleanor is a lot older than you, of course. She was married and went away from home when I was just a tiny girl. I haven't seen her all these years, and of course she's changed a great deal."

"Yes, I suppose you'd call us acquainted," answered Holt, still in that odd, hard voice. Jean felt it intuitively, but talked on, feeling her way to surer ground.

"I wonder if my sister has ever mentioned you in her letters," she said brightly. "She tells me about all the people."

"Possibly!" You could have cut ice with the sharpness of his tone. Then he added quietly:

"My name is Holt. Jasper Holt!"

He watched her with wide challenging eyes, but although

there was a puzzled look in her face the name evidently told her nothing.

"Jasper! What a beautiful name! I always thought that was the most beautiful word. The walls of the heavenly city are built of jasper, you know."

"No, I didn't know," he spoke slowly, almost worshipfully. This truly was a new kind of girl, a citizen, more like, of that heavenly city about which she spoke with such assurance as if it were an actual place, than like a mortal girl. His face was softened, made tender, as he looked at her, and saw the morning shining in her eyes. His haughtiness fell away, and all the goodness and native truth and purity that were hidden in his soul came out and sat upon his face. The people who thought they knew Jasper Holt would not have recognized him thus, walking beside the girl and looking down upon her as one looks upon the face of an angel.

Jean looked up, seeing in him only the beauty of his true self; and looking, trusted, and was not afraid.

Chapter 5

He helped her over rough places and up the steep climbs.
Hand in hand they ran down the slopes like two children out
for play; their merry laughter ringing out, forgetful of the
recent dangers through which they had passed; forgetful,
too, of perilous possibilities before them. It was enough that
the day was fresh, the sun was shining, their strength re-
newed, and they were together. Each was occupied most
with the fact of the other and the day.

They ate their berries before the heat of the noon was
fully come, and hurried on. But Holt could see that his companion was growing weary, for the excitement of the night
before had left her shaken, and more and more she faltered
and leaned heavily upon him up the hills. Then he found a
quiet resting place under some trees and bade her sleep, and
while she slept he hovered not far away.

He found a pool whereby a skill he had long practiced he
could catch some very small fish; and with due patience he
at last secured enough to make a meal. Then with infinite
pains and his knowledge of woodcraft, he accomplished a
fire once more and cooked the fish, so that when she awoke
there was dinner spread under a tree—broiled fish, with
clear water from the brook to drink.

Holt was in a hurry to get on, for he was growing uneasy
about the direction they were taking. It seemed as if they
were off the regular line of habitation and travel. Was it
possible he had turned too much to the north and was set to
enter the desert at the most remote and lonely part, where
they might travel for days without meeting anyone?

He changed the direction slightly and they started on
again, the young man watching the sun anxiously from time

to time. And now he kept the girl's arm, touching her elbow lightly to be ready with help when it was needed. Often he drew her arm within his own and fairly lifted her over hard places; and so they came to higher ground and looked out before them once more. The sun was lower now, and growing redder as it went down with premonition of the night. The man could see that the girl's steps were slower, and that her face was pale with weariness, though she said not a word and plodded cheerfully on by his side. He could see that she looked anxiously about on all sides whenever they came to the higher ground, and knew that she was thinking all this time of her mother.

The fair, weary face and bright, determined countenance touched his heart deeply, and brought out all the latent tenderness in his nature; and there arose in him a great longing to help her that made him wonder at himself.

At last as they reached another slight elevation he looked to the west and to his relief saw a small house with horses and cattle moving about in the fields. He showed it to her and her eyes lighted with joy.

"Oh, that is so good! I was worried, for I know I'm a burden. You would have gone the distance twice if you had been alone."

His hand touched her arm more reverently close.

"I am glad I was not alone," he said earnestly. "And I'm glad *you* were not alone."

She looked up to meet his eyes and there leaped from each to the other a wonderful realization of the beauty of the companionship they had held that day.

"Yes, I am glad I was not alone," she said with deep feeling, "for, oh, it would have been dreadful! And this has been ... *beautiful,*" she finished, and wondered at herself for speaking so freely. Then each was suddenly silent at the appalling realization that the free companionship of the day was almost at an end. They were coming to the world of convention and form again, where words and actions were weighed and motives questioned. There had been nothing of that here, for necessity and common peril had blotted them out of existence for the time, and it had been blessed. Now the thought came simultaneously to both. Would they ever see one another again and be friends?

The way wound down into a ravine, and the heavy growth of trees shadowed the path. It was rough and he guided her tenderly, respectfully, as one might guide a little child one loved. She felt his care in every step she took, and her heart responded gratefully to his gentleness. Her own father could not have been more thoughtful; and there was nothing familiar or presuming in his touch. He might have been a mother, the tenderness he showed. Perhaps Jean felt it more because she was so very tired, and realized her lonely position now that night was coming on again.

In the valley they came to the bank of a stream, deep and turbulent; and standing upon its brink, looking either way, they could see no possible ford. How deep it was they could not guess, but there was plainly a strong current.

Holt stood a moment, surveying the barrier to their progress, walked a few steps up the bank and down, and looked up at the westering sky. Then he deliberately walked out into the stream.

The girl on the bank caught her breath but said nothing. Must they swim across? Was there no other way? She watched Holt standing, strong and manly, in the middle of the stream, the water above his waist. Presently, when he had gone more than half way across he turned and came back to her.

She was white with excitement, but her lips were set and her eyes were bright with the intention of doing his bidding.

"I am sorry. There is no other way, and we must hurry, for the sun is getting low. We should reach that house before dark."

He stooped and gathered her in his strong arms, lifting her shoulder high, and stalked out into the stream before she knew what he was doing.

"Oh, please, I can walk as well as you," she deprecated.

"Put your arms around my neck, please," he commanded, and waded in, holding her high and dry above the water.

She obeyed instantly, in trust and shy wonder, and the water rose about them, but did not touch her.

Once, when they were in the middle of the stream, Holt's foot slipped and for an instant it seemed as though he would lose his balance, but he lifted her the higher and almost instantly recovered himself. In a moment more they had crossed the stream, and he had set her down upon the bank and was shaking the water from his garments as if it were a common thing which he had done and he enjoyed it. She looked down at herself. Not a shred of her garments was wet, while he was drenched almost to the armpits.

"You are all wet!" she exclaimed, conscience-stricken.

"You wouldn't expect me to keep dry in all that, would you?" he asked, with his eyes dancing.

Then they laughed like two children, and a frightened chipmunk ran chattering away in the trees.

"Are you all right?" he asked solicitously. "Are you perfectly dry?" His voice was husky with emotion and his eyes tender.

"Of course I'm dry," she answered dubiously, as if half-ashamed of the fact. "Why wouldn't I be when I'm treated like a baby? It seems to me, you didn't quite keep to the terms of our partnership."

"This was one of the big things," he said, "only I didn't want you to know it. To tell you the truth, I didn't know whether that stream was fordable or not; and, besides, I knew that if you got your clothes wet again it would hinder you in walking. Come, we must make that house before dark. I'm hungry, aren't you? And we're pretty sure to find bacon and cornbread at least. How does that sound?"

"Good!" she cried, laughing, and took the hand that was held out to her. Together they ran on over the rough ground toward supper and rest.

But the way was longer than they thought, and Holt had not been able to calculate on the slow steps of the girl who was unused to such long tramps, nor to going without adequate food. The sun went down and the darkness was upon them before they were anywhere near the little house.

Once Jean stumbled and almost fell, and a sound like a half sob came from her throat as she clutched at his arm to save herself. It was then he picked her up like a tired child and carried her over the rough ground, until she protested so vigorously that he was forced to set her down and both stopped to rest. For, indeed, Holt's own strength was somewhat spent by this time, though he showed no outward sign of fatigue, having been trained in a school that endures until it drops.

By this time they felt as if they had known each other for years, for there is nothing like a common peril and a common need to make souls know one another, and to bring out the true selfishness or unselfishness of each character. Because these two had been absolutely forgetful of self, each felt for the other a most extraordinary attraction and reverence.

As they sat silently under the stars, resting, it came to their minds how far from strangers they now seemed, and yet how little they knew about each other's lives; and they felt they needed not to know because of what each had been to the other during the night and the day that were passed.

When they started on their way again arm in arm, they walked silently for a time, marveling at what the day had brought them in knowledge of the other's fineness.

"I cannot be mistaken," thought Jean. "He is fine and noble ... all that a man ought to be. He looks as if he had never done anything wrong, yet is strong enough to kill the devil if he would."

By this time the little house in the distance had put a light
in its window, and guided them twinklingly to its door,
where three great dogs greeted them from afar and disputed
their entrance.

The house was not very large, only three rooms. A man
and his wife and some hired hands huddled around a kero-
sene light, the men smoking and playing cards; the wife
knitting silently in the rear.

They looked up curiously to hear the stranger's story, half
incredulous. They had not heard of any railroad accident.
They lived twenty miles from the railroad and went to town
only once a fortnight.

"This your wife?" questioned the householder of Holt.

Jean's face flamed scarlet as a new embarrassment faced
her. She had not thought of proprieties until now. Of course
they existed even in the wilderness.

Holt explained haughtily.

"Hm!" said the man still incredulous. "Anymore in your
party? Wal, my woman'll take keer your woman fer t'night,
an' in the mornin' we ken talk business. Yas, I've got horses,
but I need 'em." The man looked cunningly from one to the
other of the men.

Jean looked at Holt, and thought how far above these
people he seemed as he stood haughtily by the door in his
wet and draggled clothing, with the bearing of a young king.

"Oh, I can pay for the horses," said Holt, "and see that
they are returned, too, if that is what is the matter." And he
pulled out a roll of bills and threw several carelessly on the
table.

"Wal, that alters the case," said the man more suavely,
"of course, fer a consideration. . . ."

"Can we get some supper?" asked Holt, cutting him short.
"We've had very little to eat all day, and this lady is tired
and hungry."

The man's wife bustled forward.

"Fer land's sake!" she exclaimed, "hungry this time o'

night? We ain't got much ready, but there was some corn-bread and po'k lef' from supper, ef they'll do. The men is powah'ful eatahs."

She set out the best her house afforded, eyeing Jean's tattered silk robe enviously between trips to the cupboard. The men went on with their card game and Jean and Holt ate in silence. The girl was beginning to dread the night and to wish for the silence of the starlit world and the protection of her strong, true friend. She did not like the look of the men who fumbled the dirty cards and cast bold glances in her direction.

She was even more frightened when she learned the arrangements that were to be made for the night. She was assigned to a bunk in a small closetlike room opening from the big room in which they were all sitting. The big room, which appeared to be kitchen, parlor and dining-room combined, was to be, for that night at least, sleeping room for Holt and the other men. Several rolls of army blankets were the only visible provision made for their comfort.

Holt managed to get opportunity to whisper to her as the men were disputing over their game while the housewife retired to the guest chamber to "red up."

"Don't you worry," he reassured her softly. "I'll bunk across in front of your door. You can sleep and trust me."

She flashed up at him a bright, weary smile that sent a thrill of joy through him and made him feel that nothing in all life could be better than to defend this girl who trusted him.

In the early rose and gold of the morning Jean awoke to the smell of cooking ham and the sizzle of eggs frying just the other side of her thin partition, and knew that she had slept in safety under guard of her newfound friend.

"Jasper! Jasper Holt!" said a strange sweet voice within her soul, and she wondered at the beauty of the name and the thrill of possession she felt in it.

Jean had a little money carefully sewed inside her clothing. It was to have done for her whole western trip and bought gifts for the dear ones at home before her return. Now she realized it was her fortune. She made a bargain with the woman of the cabin for a khaki skirt and blouse, of doubtful cut and shabby mien, but whole and clean. For these she gave two dollars and the remains of the once treasured, but now tattered and travel-stained silk robe she wore. And so it was as a western girl, in riding skirt and blouse, that she emerged from the little closet where she had slept, but so wholly was she able to subjugate her clothes, and so exquisitely did her flower face and golden-brown hair set them off that they took on a style and beauty entirely out of their nature; and their former owner stared in wonder and sighed with envy as she beheld. It had not been the silken garment that made this girl a queen, but her own beauty of countenance and regal bearing; for here were her own old clothes worn like a royal robe, making the stranger lovely as the morning.

Holt looked at the girl in startled wonder when she appeared, so trim and sweet in her traveling garb, ready for the next stage of her journey, and trembled with joy at the day that was before him; albeit the end of the journey would bring sadness and parting, he knew. He wanted to knock down the men who stared insolently, offering audible comments on her complexion and bearing that made the swift, frightened color come to her cheeks. He ate his breakfast in haughty silence, sitting between Jean and one of the men, and shielding her as far as possible from any need of conversation save with her hostess who waited on them all and hovered admiringly round her young guest's chair with offers of molasses and mush that were fairly overwhelming.

"Any need fer a clergyman?" asked the ugliest of the three men, leaning forward across the table, his knife and fork held perpendicular each side of his plate, a large piece of ham aloft on his fork. He gave an ugly wink at the others and they laughed coarsely and meaningly.

"Yas, you could git the elder by goin' about ten miles out o' yer way," added another, and devoted himself audibly to his thick cup of muddy coffee.

Holt ignored these remarks and began asking questions of his host about the crops and the exact location of the house with regard to railroads, wondering meanwhile if Jean understood their rough jokes, and hoping she did not.

If she did she was serene with it all, and smiled her very sweetest on her hostess, making her heart glad at the parting by the gift of a pair of cheap, but pretty, little cuff pins that had been fastened on the front of her traveling robe.

So they mounted and rode away, Jean like the queen of a girl that she was, and her companion no less noble in his bearing. The joy they felt in the day and each other was only equaled by their own shyness in speaking of it.

Chapter 6

They talked about many things that morning as they rode happily toward Hawk Valley. Holt felt no anxiety, now, about reaching there by night, for he knew exactly where he was and how to get there. He had bargained with one of the men for firearms, and he could now shoot enough to keep them from hunger even if they were delayed. He had matches in his pocket and an old cowboy hat on his head, and he felt rested and fit for the journey. For the first half of the way, at least, he could give himself up to the bliss of a companionship such as he had never known in the whole of his young life. Reverence, awe, adoration were in his glance as he looked at the girl, and a great, wistful sadness grew as the day lingered toward evening.

They rode first straight down to the telegraph station which was about fifteen miles from the settler's cabin, and sent reassuring telegrams from the forlorn little office set out alone in the middle of the prairie; one to Jean's father and mother back in the eastern home, and one to her sister, Eleanor Harrington, in Hawk Valley.

"Don't worry about accident. Am safe and well and shall reach Hawk Valley tonight. Jean" said the first message. The second Holt worded for himself, for he had left the girl outside the station on her horse. She had asked him to be sure and tell her sister that he was with her so she would not worry, but the message he sent was:

"Safe and well, and on my way to you with a friend who will look out for me. Expect to reach Hawk Valley tonight. Jean."

Inquiry concerning the accident brought little information. The wreck had been on the "other road" and the agent "hadn't heard much." He "didn't know whether many lives were lost or not," and he "guessed it was the engineer's fault, anyhow . . . it usually was."

They rode on their way in happy converse. Jean was led to tell of her home life. Not that Holt questioned her, but she seemed to love to talk of home, and picture her family, her friends, the church where her father preached, the companions of her girlhood, the serious school life and church work to which she had been devoting herself; and, above all, he saw and wondered over the sweet confidence that existed between this girl and her parents. A wistful look came into his eyes as he thought what might have been his life if someone had cared for him and trusted in him that way; or if he had had a sister like this girl.

Suddenly, in the middle of the afternoon the girl looked up and asked: "Will your mother worry? Did you send her a telegram, too?"

He looked at her half startled.

"My mother?" he said in a strange, cold voice. "My mother never worries about me. She isn't that kind. I doubt if she even knows where I am these days. I've been west for a long time. Father died and mother married again since I left home. I don't suppose she would even hear of the accident. There's no one to care where I am." There was a bitterness in the young voice and a hardness on the handsome features that cast a pall over the beauty of the afternoon for Jean.

"Oh," she said, looking at him earnestly. "Oh, don't say that! I'm sure someone cares."

There were tears in her eyes. He looked so noble and good to her, and her heart went out to him utterly in his loneliness. In that moment she knew that she cared with all her heart; that she would always care. It was a strange and wonderful feeling.

He looked at her with wonder again and a yearning that he could not hide.

"I believe *you* would care!" he exclaimed.

She smiled through a sudden mist of tears.

"Yes, I should care, I couldn't help it," she said. "You have done so much for me you know, and I *know* you so well. . . ." She hesitated. "I don't see how anybody who belonged to you could help caring." Her cheeks were rosy with the effort to say what she meant without seeming forward.

His brow darkened.

"Belonged!" he said bitterly. "Belonged! Yes, that's it. I don't belong! I don't belong anywhere!"

His voice was so different and so harsh that it almost frightened her. She watched him, half afraid as he brought his horse to a sudden stop and looked about him. Then he changed the subject abruptly.

"This is a good place to camp for supper and rest," he said, as if he had quite forgotten what they had been saying.

He swung down from the saddle, hobbled his horse, and came around to her side to help her alight; but stood a moment looking earnestly, tenderly into her eyes, and she looked back at him trustingly, wonderingly with the worshipful homage a woman's eyes can hold for the man who has won her tenderest thoughts. She did not know she was looking that way. She would have been filled with confusion if she had known it. It was unconscious and the man knew so and treasured her look the more for that.

"I believe you do care, now," he said in a voice filled with a sort of holy awe that made the girl's heart leap up and the color flame into her cheeks.

Then before she could answer or think to be embarrassed, he lifted her reverently from the saddle and put her on the ground.

He hobbled her horse, unstrapped the pack of provisions and went off to gather firewood, but when he returned she was sitting where he put her under the tree, her face buried in her hands, her slender form motionless.

He stood for a moment and watched her, then came over and knelt down beside her, and taking her hands gently from her face, looked into the dewy depths of her sweet eyes and spoke.

"Don't!" he pleaded gently. "Let's have supper now, and then we'll talk it all out. Will you come and help me make a fire?"

There was something in his strong, tender glance that helped her to rise to his call. A lovely smile grew in her eyes. She let him help her to her feet, and casting aside the reserved shyness that had fallen over her like a misty veil, she ran here and there, gathering sticks and helping to make the fire blaze; talking merrily about the supper they were preparing just as she had done all day; but her heart was in a tumult of wonder.

Holt shot a couple of rabbits and put them to roast before the fire. Jean set herself to toast the soggy cornbread and make it more palatable. Their merry laughter rang out again and again as they prepared their simple meal. They were like two children playing house. No one looking on would have seen any difference in their demeanor from what it had been all day. It was only when Holt was out in the open, shooting rabbits, that he allowed the sadness and gloom to settle down upon his young face. It was only when he was away gathering more wood that Jean, left to watch the sputtering rabbits, let the cornbread burn, while her face grew thoughtful, and her eyes sweet with a tender light.

It was when the supper was eaten and the fire flickering low in the dying light of sunset that Holt came and sat down beside the girl, and again a great silence fell between them.

Holt had planned their homecoming to be in the dark. For the girl's sake he would not have witnesses to their arrival. This thoughtfulness sprang from finer feelings than the people of Hawk Valley dreamed that he possessed. There remained but a little over an hour's ride now to reach Hawk Valley, and Holt did not mean they should get there before nine o'clock at the earliest.

He sat gravely quiet, his strong hands folded across his

raised knees, his back against a tree, looking bravely, wistfully, off into the distance. He seemed a great deal older, now, with that grave, sad expression. Jean stole a glance at him now and then, as she plucked at the vegetation about her, and wondered why this appalling silence, which she seemed powerless to break, had so suddenly fallen upon them.

Then the man's voice broke the stillness in a low tense tone. "There's something I must tell you."

The very air seemed waiting to hear what he would say. The girl scarcely breathed.

"It wouldn't have been the square thing for me to tell you that I loved you if I had been the only one that cared; but we've been through all this together, and it's as if we had known each other for years . . . and . . . *you care too!* I can see it in your eyes. I'm not worthy of it . . . but you care . . . and it's up to me to help you stop it. It would be an easier job, perhaps, if I were used to being trusted, but it's an honest fact that you're the first respectable person who has really trusted me since I can remember, and it comes hard. . . ."

His voice broke as if an alien sob had wandered into his bronzed throat. A sob swelled in the girl's throat, too, and her little briar-scratched hand stole out and just touched his arm reassuringly with a feather glance of pressure, and withdrew as if to say, "I will bear my part of this trouble, whatever it is. Please don't suffer more than your own part."

He turned at that and the cloud on his face cleared and brightened into a smile that seemed to enfold her in his glance of tenderness, yet he lifted not a finger to touch her.

"I love you! *How* I love you!" he said, in a low, lingering tone, as if the speaking of the words were exquisite joy that he knew was fleeting and must be treasured.

"I never knew there was a girl like you. I loved you at once as soon as I saw you on the train . . . but I knew, of course, you were not for me. I'm not fit for you . . . I'm not in your class at all ... and I wouldn't have dreamed of anything but worshiping you, even after these days together ... only you *care!* You trust me! That broke me all up! I'd give anything in this world if I could keep that and take it to the end and die with it ... to remember that look in your eyes when you said you trusted me ... and thought I was good ... and all. If you weren't going right where they know all about me and will tell you, I'd never have opened my lips. I'd have stolen this one little bit of trust and kept it for my own; for down in my heart I know it isn't wrong, I know you *may* trust me. I'd give my life to keep that trust. . . ."

He was looking straight into her clear eyes as he talked and his own eyes were clear and good, showing his strong, true spirit at its best. The appeal in his voice suddenly went to the girl's heart. With a growing uneasiness she had listened to his words, and she felt that she could bear no more. The tears rushed to her eyes and she put up her hands to cover her face.

"Please. Tell me quick!" she breathed softly.

Puzzled, thrilled with the wonder of her tears, and longing inexpressibly to comfort her, he put out his hand awkwardly and laid it on her bowed head bending over her as he might have done to a child in trouble.

"There's nothing for you to feel bad about," he said in a voice of wonderful tenderness. "I'm bearing this circumstance. I just wanted to be the one to tell you myself that I'm not what you think me. I'm not bad, really, the way I might be, but I've not been good, and I'm not a gentleman, not the kind you're used to. Nobody thinks I'm worth anything at all. Your people hate me, and would think it a good thing if somebody would kill me, I know. You see how it is that I can't be like other men who love you. I cannot ask you to marry me; for after you've heard what your family will say about me you won't look at me yourself ... and I don't blame you. It's all my own fault, I suppose. I can see it now, though I never thought so till I looked into your eyes on the train. If I had known a girl like you was coming my way, I'd have made things different ... I'd have been ready ... but I didn't know. Nobody ever told me! And now it's too late. I'm not worthy of you."

He took his hand from her head and dropped back against the tree again, a bitter expression on his face.

"Oh, don't," she pleaded softly, quick to see his changing mood. "Please don't look like that. Won't you tell me what you have done that makes them all feel so about you?"

There was silence for a moment between them while the twilight grew luminous with the coming of a pale, young moon battling with the dying ruby of the sun. So, in the holy of the evening he came to his confession, face to face with his sins before the pure eyes of the girl he loved.

Chapter 7

The stars were large and vivid above them, like capers of tall angels bent to light a soul's confession up to God.

The beautiful silence that brooded over the plain was broken now and again by distant calls of some wild creature, but that only emphasized the stillness and the privacy of the night.

The two whose souls were thus come so strangely and unexpectedly into a common crisis of their lives sat awed and stricken before the appalling irrevocableness of deeds that are past.

Jasper Holt broke the silence at last.

"I was never as bad as they thought I was," he said in a broken voice, though there was no hint in it of attempting to discount his blame. "They laid a lot of things at my door that I never thought of doing . . . some things I would have scorned to do." His voice was haughty now with pride. "I suppose it was my fault they thought I did them. I *let* them think so. I grew to glory in their thinking so, and sometimes helped it on just for the pleasure of feeling that they, through their injustice, were more in the wrong than I. I suppose I had no right to do that. At least I see now that for . . . your sake . . . I should have kept my record clear." He lifted his gray eyes in the starlight to her face for one swift look and then went on.

"It was none of their business what I did though, and my theory always has been to do as I pleased so long as I lived up to my creed. For I had a creed, a kind of religion, if you want to call it that. Put into a single word, perhaps nine-tenths of my creed is independence. What people thought of me didn't come into my scheme of life. I thought it a slavery to bow to public opinion, and gloried in my freedom. It seemed a false principle without cause or reason. You see I never reckoned on your coming. I thought I was living my life just for myself. I can see now that underneath all the falseness of the world's conventionalities there runs some good reason, and there may be circumstances where some of the things they insist upon are right . . . even necessary. This is one. I never considered anything like this. I couldn't see any reason why I should ever need to care what people thought of me, or to go out of my way to make them think well of me. I always relied on something else to get me what I wanted, and so far it has not failed. *They* will tell you that. They will let you know that I have not been powerless because some men hated me—for though they have hated me they have also feared me."

The girl turned her eyes, tear-filled and full of amazement, to look at him, studying the fine outline of features against the starlit background of the sky. She could see the power in his face; power with gentleness was what she had seen when she first looked at him; but hate! Fear! How could men so misjudge him? What was there about him to fear?

He read her thought.

"You don't see how that could be," he said sadly. "I don't look that way to you now. But wait till you hear them talk. You'll get another viewpoint. You won't see me this way at all anymore. You'll see me with their eyes."

"Don't!" she said with a sob in her voice, putting up her hands as if to defend herself from his words.

"I shall not blame you," he said bending tenderly, eagerly toward her. "It will not be your fault. It will be almost inevitable. You belong with them and not with me, and you cannot help seeing me that way when you get with them. It is a part of my miserable folly. It is my punishment. I have no right to make you think I am better than they believe. It will be easier for you to forget me if you believe what they do."

"I will *never* believe what they do!" said the girl vehemently. "I will never listen to their opinion! You may have sinned; you may have done a lot of things that you ought not to have done—I am not wise to judge those things—but you are *not bad! I know* you are not! And I know I can trust you! I shall always trust you no matter what anybody says, no matter how things look! I *know* you are good and true! *I know you!*"

She put out her hands piteously toward him and her delicate face was lifted with determination and intensity. There was something glorious in the sparkle of her eyes. He took her hands reverently.

"You *dear!*" he breathed tenderly. "You wonderful woman!"

She caught her breath and her hands trembled in his, but she sat up proudly as if she were defying the world in his defense.

"Now, tell me the rest," she said. "Tell it *all!* And then I shall believe just what you tell me, nothing more! If they tell me other things I shall know they are false. I shall not be afraid when you tell me what you have done because you are here and I can look into your eyes and know you are sorry; so tell me the worst. But you needn't ever think I shall listen to *them.*"

So, with her soft small hands in his, and her eyes bright as the stars above them, looking straight into his, he looked back as straightforwardly and told her. All the foolishness, the stubbornness, and independence. All the fight against convention and law. His gambling and wild, rough living. His companioning with men who were outlaws and sinners. His revolutionary methods of dealing with those who did not do as he thought they ought, or who tried to interfere with him. His summary punishment of those who stirred his soul to wrath. He told it in low tones and grave, searching out each confession of his heart as though he would make a clean sweep of it, and lifting his eyes bravely each time to meet the pain he could not help seeing in hers. It was his real judgment, his first sense of shame and sorrow and repentance.

And then when it was told he bowed his head in silence for a moment, still holding her hands, as though there yet remained something more to say. At last he spoke.

"There's one thing," he said, and he lifted his head with a sigh. "Yes, two things, I might say that I suppose you'll be glad to hear. I haven't been a drinking man! I doubt if many of your friends will believe that, for I'm often in the saloons, and with men who drink. I haven't noised it abroad that I don't drink, and only those who have been with me a good deal and know my ways, understand it. I simply don't drink because I don't want to. I saw what it did to men when I first came out here. I knew I needed my brains for what I wanted to do, and I didn't like the idea of surrendering them for a few hours' carouse and putting myself even temporarily out of my own control, so I just determined I wouldn't drink and I didn't. But your brother-in-law and sister won't believe that. My reputation is understood to be of the worst, and drinking is a matter of course when one is hard and wild as they think I am. There's another thing, too. I've kept away from women. Some of them hurt me too much when I was a kid, and when I grew a little older, I decided against them all. That's kept me clean. I can look you in the eyes and not be ashamed. I didn't do it because I had any idea there would ever be one like you in my world. I did it just because the kind of thing that some men liked, turned me sick to think of. This is probably another thing your people wouldn't believe. They've heard otherwise of me. They've shouldered every crime in the calendar on me. And perhaps they've had some reason from their standpoint. I haven't always tried to make things look right. I didn't care. It wasn't their business. There was a girl came to the Valley once with a traveling show. She was down on her luck and just about ready to give up and take her own life. I helped her out a bit, paid for her at the hotel a few days till she got rested, and sent her on her way to her father in Missouri; but you ought to have heard the rumpus the town raised! That added to my unsavory reputation, you see. Well, I'm no saint, but I've kept clean! So, there you have the worst of me—and the best—but it's bad enough. Your father wouldn't stand for me a minute, and I guess he's right. I don't blame him. I blame myself. As for your sister! Why, if Harrington knew I was out here alone with you he'd bring a posse of men and shoot me on the spot for daring to bring you home. He would. He feels just that way about me."

"I shall change all that," said Jean with a thrill in her voice. "I shall tell them how mistaken they have been in you. I shall tell them that was only a kind of rough outside that you wore—a mask that hid your inner feelings. I shall make them understand that they have not known the real man you are at all."

"You cannot do that, little girl," said the man, gently leaning toward her. "It would be best for you not to try. I tell you, you do not know in the least what the feeling is against me."

"But you will help to show them, too," said Jean, wide-eyed with sorrow. "You will not go on doing those things . . . those . . . well . . . the things that made them feel you were not right. . . ." She paused in a confusion of words, not liking to voice a thought against him. "You will not do so anymore?" She pleaded wistfully like a child. "You will make them see, for my sake if not for your own, how wonderful you are! How fine you have been to me! You will not let them go on thinking. *You will change it all?*"

Her voice choked off in a sob and for a moment she dropped her tear-wet face down upon his hands that held hers. The strong man thrilled and trembled with her touch and it was then he felt the most crucial moment of his punishment.

He sat white and silent for a moment, longing to gather her into his arms and comfort her, to crush her to him; but he would not. The nobleness in him held her sacred because he knew he was unworthy. Then he spoke in a low, grave tone, and his voice had a hollow, hopeless sound.

"I'll change, of course," he said. "I couldn't do otherwise. Did you think I could go on that way after having known you? I never could do any of the things again that I know you wouldn't like. I couldn't, now that you've trusted me. I wouldn't *want* to. You have made everything seem different. If it'll please you any I'll promise anything you like. But of course I know that doesn't matter so far as our ever having each other is concerned. Nothing I can do can make people forget what they think I am. They would never feel differently. They would feel it a disgrace for you to speak to me. They'd always think you'd gone to perdition if you had anything to do with me. I'm not fit for you. I know it and there's an end of it, but I'll spend the rest of my life trying to make myself what I ought to have been, if that will comfort you any."

The girl's hands clung now with almost a painful clasp, and tears were dropping down her face.

"Don't! *Don't!*" he pleaded earnestly. "Don't take it so. I'm not worth it, really I'm not. You'll find it out when you get to your sister's and hear her talk, and *forget* about this." His voice broke and he lifted his face, white with sudden realization of what that would mean to him. "Oh, God! What a fool I have been!" The words were wrung from the depths of his soul.

Then the girl spoke, her voice calm with a suddenly acquired strength.

"Listen!" she said, and he wondered at her quietness. "*I* shall *never* forget. *Never!* Nothing that anybody can say will ever make me think as they do of you. I *know* you and you have saved my life."

He stirred impatiently, and almost roughly tried to draw his hands away.

"Don't talk of gratitude," he said huskily.

"No," she said firmly, taking his hands again and laying her own within them as before. Then he accepted them as if they were a sacred trust, folding his reverently about them.

"I am not talking of gratitude," she said, and her voice was tense with feeling. "You saved my life and I know what you are, and what you have done for me. Nothing can ever change that, not even what you have done in the past; and nobody can ever make me feel differently about you. I know you, I trust you . . . I *love you!*" Her voice was low and sweet as she said this and she did not lift her eyes. The young man felt her fingers tremble within his own strong grasp, and he looked down wonderingly at the slender wrists and thrilled with holy awe at her words. It humbled him, shamed him, with a pain that was a solemn joy, to hear her. And he had nothing to say. What gracious influence had been at work in his behalf that a miracle so great should have been wrought in a pure girl's heart for him? He was an outlaw: a careless, selfish, wild man who had hitherto lived as he pleased, for himself, caring for nobody, nobody caring for him. He had held his head high and gone his independent way. He had held the creed that the whole world was against him, and his chief aim in life should be to circumvent and annoy that world. Nothing good and holy had ever come into his life before. Knowledge he had, and a certain amount of worldly wisdom learned in a hard school, and well learned; but love, care, tenderness, trust had never been given to him even in his babyhood. No wonder he was confounded at the sudden treasure thrust upon him.

"I am only a very young girl," Jean's voice went on. "I know you are right that I must not do anything to distress my father and mother. They love me very much and I love them. You and I can go our separate ways if we must, but nobody can hinder me from trusting you. It is right I should. I owe it to you for what you have done for me. And my love I could not help giving you. I know you are going to be right and true forever; I know you will not do those things any-

more that have made people think you were not good. I
know you will always be just what I think you are now,
won't you?"

His voice was low and solemn, and his eyes held depths
of sincerity as he lifted them to her pleading ones and
answered.

"I promise you."

"And I promise you that I will trust you always," she said,
and thus their covenant was made.

For a long moment they sat with clasping hands, unaware
of the beauty of the evening, aware only of their own two
startled, suffering spirits, that had found and lost each other
and learned the consequences of sin. They did not seem to
need words, for each knew what was in the other's heart.

He raised her at last to her feet and, bending low, whispered:

"I thank you."

He stood a moment hesitating, then gave her hands one
quick pressure again and turned away.

"I was going to ask something," he said, "but I guess that
isn't square."

And she stood pondering what it might have been.

Silently he helped her on the pony and without words
they rode away into the moonlight.

There were tears in the girl's eyes when she lifted them at
last and asked, "And won't I see you at all? Won't you ever
come to the house?"

There was a sound almost of tears in the man's voice as he
answered:

"I am afraid not."

After that they talked softly in tones that people use when
they are about to go apart on a long journey and may not
ever meet again. Monosyllables, half-finished sentences, of
which each knew the beginning or the ending without the
words. Large understanding, quick pain, wistfulness, longing, a question now and then—this was their conversation.

They came at last to the brow of a hill where below them at a gentle slope Hawk Valley lay, its lights twinkling among the velvety shadows of the night. In the clear moonlight it seemed so near, so sudden, as it lay just below them that Jean caught her breath in a cry that was almost a sob. She knew without being told that the parting of their ways had come. By common consent they checked their horses and made them stand side by side. Holt put out his hand and laid it on hers.

"Don't!" he said huskily. "I won't disappoint you. No matter what anybody tells you, always remember that. I won't disappoint you! You needn't think I've forgotten or changed. I can't forget the only good thing that ever came into my life. *You can trust me!*"

"I know," she replied softly. "I know I can trust you. And I've been thinking. There's no reason why you couldn't come to see me. I don't care what anybody thinks. You saved my life! I'm not ashamed of you. I have the right to ask you to call and to receive you. My father would approve of that, I am sure."

"You're wonderful!" he exclaimed intensely. "You're not like any other girl I ever saw. But, it wouldn't do. Your father might stand for it, but your brother-in-law never would. He hates me like poison, not so much because of my reputation as because I've stood in the way of some of his plans. He would kick me out like a dog if I darkened his doors. You'll understand when you hear them talk. It would be just as well if you didn't say anything about me. It won't be necessary for them to know who brought you home; just say a man who was on the train."

Jean straightened up in her saddle and grasped his hand.

"Indeed I shall tell them who brought me out of death, and just what I think of him. They shall know all that you have done for me. Do you think I would keep still about it? I couldn't. It would be disloyalty. It would be cowardly!"

He watched her sweet face and flashing eyes in the moonlight and hungrily stored the picture away in his memory.

"Darling!" he breathed reverently, as if the words were drawn from his lips in spite of all resolution. Then he raised his voice a trifle, and lifted his head to the night sky.

"I never knew a girl could be like this! What a fool I have been!" The words ended almost in a groan, and for answer the girl drew nearer to him and laid her other hand gently upon his.

Lights flashed below them in the village and voices rose; a coarse laugh rang out and a child's cry; some people talked in an open doorway in another place and called goodnight. Then a door slammed and other lights twinkled: just the commonplace noises of life jarring in to break a moment of tremendous import in the lives of these two. The time had come to go down to their valley and they knew it. With one lingering handclasp they started on down to the village.

Holt selected the shadowed ways and quieter approach to the Harrington home, and the two rode silently until they came to the house.

Chapter 8

Holt checked the horses and, dismounting, stood beside Jean in the shadow of a great tree by the roadside. Within ten feet of them the light from a wide window streamed out upon the grass in front of a pleasant house built in bungalow style, with broad porches and vine-clad approaches. Hammocks and easy rockers were dimly visible, with a brighter hint of glow and warmth inside the swaying curtains of the window where a piano was sounding pleasantly, and a man and woman were sitting on either side of a table under a prettily shaded reading lamp. A boy's voice called down the stairs and the little girl at the piano stopped playing and answered him; then tinkled on with her music.

All this the two under the tree saw and heard without sensing it. They were looking into one another's eyes in the semi-darkness, realizing that across that streak of light was separation for them, perhaps forever; and that probably this instant here and now was all that was left to them together out of the eternity of the future years.

Jean put her hands timidly on Holt's shoulders. "I've been thinking what it was you wanted to ask of me," she said so softly that if one had been passing it would have seemed but the breathing of the evening air. She waited and Holt looked at her wistfully.

"I have no right," he said. "It wouldn't be square."

The girl's eyes looked steadily, shyly into his, though in the shadow they could see more with the spirit than with the material vision.

"Was it . . ." she stopped, her heart beating fast. "Was it this?"

She leaned forward and kissed him softly on the forehead

just where the soft curls waved away; and her lips were like a benediction, that seemed to bring forgiveness and a purging away of the past.

With bowed head as at a sacrament he stood, then softly said, "You have understood, and I thank you. I had no right to ask, but I can never forget or be false to that."

He stooped and laid his lips reverently on her hands; then lifted her down quickly as if he could not bear to make the sorrow of the parting longer; and together they went forward across the patch of light, up the path and the wide low steps to the porch.

Holt knocked once on the door, not loudly, but there was in the sound a menace that made Jean shudder as she heard it. She reached out her hand to his as if she would take shelter there from something that was coming, that she could not quite understand. Holt pressed her fingers quickly, tightly in a clasp that almost hurt her, and then dropping her hand, stepped back into the shadow of the vines as the tinkling piano stopped. There was a sound of footsteps coming to the door, and of voices in expectation.

The door was flung wide and in the stream of light Mr. and Mrs. Harrington stood looking eagerly out into the darkness, with a little girl of twelve in a white dress, peering shyly but curiously around her mother and a boy of five struggling to get into the center of the family group. Jean stood alone in the light on the porch, with Holt in the shadow at her side.

"I have brought Miss Grayson," said Holt in a grave, almost challenging tone, from his dark position just outside the stream of light.

But the people in the doorway whose eyes had come from the lighted room saw only the figure of the girl standing in the brightness.

"Oh, Jean! My little sister! You have come at last!" cried Mrs. Harrington, rushing forward to clasp her in her arms, and draw her inside the door; and in the confusion of the greetings the girl's escort was quite forgotten for the moment.

Within the doorway at last they looked about for him and found no one.

"Why, who came with you, child? Where has he gone?" asked her brother-in-law solicitously. "We must ask him in and hear all about your adventures." He stepped out on the porch and looked down the path in the moonlight, but saw no one anywhere.

"Yes, please ask him in," pleaded Jean, her face illumined with eagerness. "He has been so wonderful! He saved my life. If it hadn't been for him I shouldn't have been here." And she hurried to the door and peered out into the darkness.

"Of course," said her sister, going to the door to look. "How thoughtless of us not to have welcomed him at once, but we were so overwhelmed to have you at last, after all the anxiety. You can't think how terrible it has been. Which way could he have gone, James? Look down the road either way. He can't be far away. What was his name, Jean? Can't you call after him?"

"He must be over there." Jean pointed toward the great tree where the horses had stood but a short moment before. "We dismounted just under that tree. He can't have gone far with two horses so soon . . ." and she hurried across the grass to the tree, but there was no sign of horse or man in the deep shadow or the serene moonlight anywhere.

"Call, James!" commanded Mrs. Harrington, and her husband obeyed, but no answering call came back, save the echoes of his voice.

"What did you say his name was, Jean?" asked the puzzled householder walking slowly back to the steps. "It seems very strange he could get away so soon. Where was he going? Did he live near here? We ought to put him up for the night, of course. It's most mortifying to have him disappear in this manner when he has been so good to you. He must have gone to find rest and food for his horses and himself. I'll send the servant out to look him up. He'll surely find him. What did he look like? What did you say was his name?"

Jean, slowly climbing the steps to the porch, and comprehending that Holt's disappearance had been intentional, answered in a strange low voice that tried to be natural.

"Holt, his name was Holt, Jasper Holt." Her voice lingered on the words as if she would glorify the man by merely speaking his name, and elevate him in their eyes to the place he occupied in her heart.

"Holt!" exclaimed her brother-in-law. "Holt! Not Jasper Holt! Impossible! There must be some mistake."

"It couldn't have been Jasper Holt, of course," said his wife quite decidedly. "He isn't capable of saving anybody's life, much less a relative of ours, Jean, dear. It *must* have been someone else. Are you sure about the name?"

"Quite sure!" said Jean composedly, though she felt her whole frame trembling.

"Perhaps it was his father," suggested Eleanor, looking at her husband. "Have you ever heard that Jasper Holt had a father living, James? How old a man was he, Jean?"

"He was a young man, Eleanor, tall and handsome, and very brave and strong." Jean's eyes were lifted to meet her sister's smiling doubt, and her chin was raised with an attitude of defiance.

"Listen, Eleanor, he was wonderful. I dropped from the window of the burning sleeper into a river, and something struck me on the head when I rose and tried to swim."

"You poor, dear little girl!" interpolated Eleanor, reaching out yearning arms to clasp her sister again, but Jean held her gently back and went on with her eager tale.

"He caught me and dragged me along, helping me as far as I could go, and when I couldn't swim any longer he brought me a long distance himself to land, and carried me a great ways through the woods. He built a fire, dried his own coat, and put it over me while I slept. He took care of me just as my own father might have done; found food, water, and a house where we slept the first night; and where we got horses. He has been splendid to me all day."

"Well, he can't be our Jasper Holt, dear, it's impossible. He isn't a bit like that."

"Yes," said Jean, looking earnestly, bravely at her sister. "Yes, Eleanor, it is your Jasper Holt. He told me you did not like him, but I'm sure you don't know what he really is or you couldn't, you *couldn't* possibly think ill of him. Oh, Eleanor!" and suddenly Jean's courage gave way in a flood of tears and she threw herself in her sister's arms.

"You poor, dear little girl! You are all worn out and we are letting you stand here and talk when you ought to be in bed this minute," exclaimed her sister, folding her in loving arms. "Never mind now, dear, you just forget it till tomorrow. It was an awful experience for you to go through all alone with a strange man, and you need a lot of rest before you can tell us about it. Come now, James will send the man out to hunt for your escort and you needn't worry anymore. We shall find out there is some mistake. I'm sure the Jasper Holt we know would never turn out of his way to save anybody's life—he'd much rather kill someone—unless he had some evil purpose in it. It's possibly someone who has used his name for fun or something. Come now, Jean dear, take off your hat. Why, child, where did you get this ridiculous rig you have on? It's good it wasn't daylight when you arrived. It was thoughtful of your escort to bring you in the dark. Your trunk arrived yesterday. Come up to your room and wash while I have your supper put on the table. I've kept it nice and hot for I knew you would be hungry."

Jean suddenly lifted up her head and wiped the tears away.

"I'd like to tell you just a little first, if you please," she said. "It's no use whatever for you to send out to find Mr. Holt. He will not come back, I am sure. I suppose he meant to slip away. He told me before he got here that you would not want him. He did not want me to mention him at all, but I had to tell you how fine he has been."

Mrs. Harrington and her husband stood looking at one another aghast; while Jean, her hair dishevelled, her sweet face glowing with eagerness, sketched most briefly but forcibly the peril through which she had come and the faithfulness and care of her protector. More than one glance of incredulity passed between husband and wife as the girl went on with her story; and yet, as she came to her final sentences, they perceived that her protector and savior must have been the Jasper Holt they knew and despised.

"I guess it was Holt all right!" said Harrington, with an ominous frown, "and he did well to disappear like the coward that he is. He knew he was not wanted around here!"

"Coward?" exclaimed Jean, "coward! Jasper Holt is no coward! You do not know him!" Her eyes were flashing fire; her whole slender body tense with indignation.

Eleanor looked alarmedly at her husband, but tried to smile pacifically at her sister. "Never mind tonight, dear," she said soothingly, "he's evidently appeared to you as an angel of light. He *is* handsome, I must admit—in a kind of a dashing, dreadful way—and of course *any*one who saved you and was kind to you would be under a kind of glamour just now. I'm sure we're grateful to him for not letting you drown. It's quite the unexpected; but really, when it comes to bringing you home, you're quite attractive, you know; and I've no doubt he thought it would be pleasant to have a little flirtation with a pretty girl. Besides, I think he rather enjoyed putting James under an obligation to him. I only hope he will know enough not to presume upon this for further acquaintance. He has been most unpleasant, not to say criminal, in a business way. But never mind now, Jean, we'll talk about it more tomorrow. Wait until you hear what everybody says about him and then you will see we are not prejudiced. We don't blame you for being grateful. Be as grateful as you like, but *don't have anything more to do with him!* Come now, this is the way to your room. Let me help you unfasten this ridiculous frock. Where did you say you got it? I know you never had this in your wardrobe when you started from home and Mother. . . ."

Mrs. Harrington chattered on, giving the girl time to recover her calmness, for she saw that she was terribly excited; and Jean choked back the hot tears that welled to her eyes, and the words of protest against the injustice to Holt, and went about her toilet.

In a few minutes more she had made a hasty toilet and, attired in one of her own cool little muslins, she was seated in the dining room with an admiring audience about her asking questions about home, the journey and the cousins she had visited on the way. The children hung about her eagerly, patting her shyly, and watching her every move with shining eyes. Almost, for a few minutes, the girl forgot the perils through which she had passed, and the man of whom she must not speak.

When supper was finished and the children were sent to bed, Jean suddenly remembered the leather case she had been charged to convey to her brother-in-law.

"Oh, James," she said, "I've a package for you; 'very important papers' the old man who gave it to me said they were. He was going to get off at the next station, he said—he had been telegraphed for, or something—and he heard me tell the conductor that you had telegraphed for a berth for me, so he asked if I would give you these papers at once. If he knows about the accident, he's worrying about his precious bundle by this time, I suspect. Wait, I'll get it. It's upstairs in my bag."

Jean hurried up to her room and had a little difficulty in finding the bag which she finally discovered under a trunk tray. The sight of the little wax paper cups and her own little damp wad of a handkerchief she and Holt had both used for a towel that afternoon when they washed their hands at a spring, struck a pang to her heart. The dampness and stuffed condition of the bag made it difficult to get the bundle out, and giving it an impatient jerk she turned the whole thing upside down on the little table that stood by the bedside. The bundle rolled to the floor, opening as it fell, for the edges of the leather case had loosened with the wetting they had received, and let out the papers that it held. Jean stooped wearily and gathered them up with a gingerly touch, remembering the uncouth old man who had given it to her, and was rather surprised that the papers themselves looked clean and were evenly folded. She hurried them down to the bright living room, holding them out to Mr. Harrington, and was startled at the look on his face as he saw what she gave him.

"You needn't be afraid, it's not a ghost," she laughed as she put the damp package in his hand. "It's rather dilapidated, but it's all there. I did the best I could with it, but it was submerged for a long time, and I had no opportunity to dry it."

Harrington said nothing, but his face turned suddenly white and his hand shook as he turned back the limp leather and looked at the folded papers inside. She saw by his expression that he knew what it was.

"Are they so very important?" she asked.

"Pretty important," he said briefly, opening the papers one at a time and half turning away from her as if he did not wish her to see them.

"I'm glad I saved them, then," she said fervently. "I came near to throwing them away when I dropped out of that window. The old man was so dirty I couldn't bear to have anything he had handled. Well, goodnight."

She turned away, feeling that he wished to be alone with the papers, but he looked up and called her back.

"Wait, Jean. What kind of a looking man was it who gave them to you?"

She told him in detail.

"Did you let anyone see this case?" he asked sharply.

"No," said Jean, and then remembered. "Well, not exactly. It fell out of my bag once and the paper I had wrapped it in fell off, but there was no one by but Mr. Holt and he didn't notice it in the least."

"Are you sure?" questioned her brother-in-law, his face white, his expression growing tense with anxiety. "How near was he?"

"He was standing close by, not three feet away, and he stooped and picked up the case and handed it back to me without saying a word," said Jean, a hint almost of indignation in her tone that warned her brother-in-law he had gone far enough in his inquiries.

"Well, never mind," he said, turning away. "It's all right, of course. They are very important papers relating to some business my company is carrying on, and Holt has been making a good deal of trouble for us. I would rather he didn't know about them."

Jean was vexed, she scarcely knew why, and stood for an instant hesitating. Should she say more or go immediately upstairs? It was very strange for James to act that way, as if it were her fault. And it was most unreasonable and unjust for him to feel that way about Jasper Holt. Her soul revolted against it.

Harrington looked up, annoyed, as if he would be rid of the girl; and then, realizing the look of wonder on her face, he tried to control his expression and smile.

"Well, goodnight, Jean. Don't let this trouble you. I'm deeply grateful that you were so faithful as to guard the papers through all your experiences. Rest well and don't think anymore about it."

So dismissed, the girl turned slowly and mounted the

stairs, but as she glanced back she saw him fluttering the papers over as if he were counting them two or three times. As she reached the landing she heard him summon a servant and send him in hot haste for someone named "Garrett."

"Tell him he must come at once, it is important, urgent business," was the message sent. Then she closed her door and went about her preparations for the night, but her mind was strangely disturbed.

Chapter 9

Eleanor Harrington came presently to the door and tapped.

"You're not asleep yet, are you, Jean?" she called. "James just wanted me to ask if there was any possibility that some of those papers were lost on the way? Did they fall or did anything happen where one might have slipped out? He thinks that two most important ones are missing."

"Not while they were in my possession, Eleanor," said Jean positively, feeling a return of her annoyance at her brother-in-law's manner. She opened the door and stood framed in the doorway, looking adorable in her little pale blue kimono, with her hair tumbling about her shoulders. The elder sister bent down and kissed her affectionately.

"You poor little girl, how tired you look. Get to bed quickly. It was a shame to trouble you anymore about those horrid papers. Goodnight, dear! This is positively my last appearance," and she closed the door and went downstairs.

Five minutes later Jean turned to put out the light and saw, lying on the floor on the farther side of the little bedstand, a slip of paper folded once across, and about the size of the wallet which she had given her brother-in-law. She pounced upon it and took it nearer the light. It looked more like an old letter that might have slipped from her trunk tray than a business paper.

As she opened the paper the name of Jasper Holt caught her eye, and her interest was at once enlisted. How came a paper bearing that name in the guest chamber of her brother-in-law's house? It could not possibly have come through her. Nothing of his could have caught in her garments, there was no place for anything to catch, and no way that his possession could get into her bag. It could not, of course, be the missing paper from the wallet, since it bore his hated name. Yet, her brother-in-law had spoken of disagreeable business relations. Would this paper, perhaps, by any chance, explain to her the animosity that had sprung up between the two men? She felt she had the right to know. She glanced quickly down the page.

It was a simple contract, the grant of certain water rights to Jasper Holt in consideration of payment received, and to the smallest child who could read at all it would be patent that the paper must be the private property of Jasper Holt himself. How came it here in the house of his enemy?

She read the few lines over many times, until she knew them thoroughly; and slowly there grew in her heart a conviction that something was wrong somewhere. Her first impulse, to call her sister and consult her, she could not bring herself to follow. It seemed, somehow, that here was something she must think out for herself.

However and whatever her brother-in-law and sister felt, *she* owed a loyalty to Jasper Holt. She might not do a wrong, even inadvertently, to him who had saved her life and cared for her so tenderly. If he were here she would unquestioningly have put the paper into his hands and asked him what to do about it. She had promised to trust him, and she felt such great confidence in him, from what she already knew about him, that she was convinced he would send the paper back to Harrington if it belonged to the latter.

But Holt was not here, and the problem of the future was still shrouded in difficulty. Would she ever see him to consult? Was this, perhaps, one of the missing papers James wanted, and why did she not trust James to give it back to Holt as quickly as she would have trusted Holt to give it to James? The question brought a look of trouble to her brow, and a flush to her cheek. Did she distrust her brother-in-law just a little bit? Had she always done so without knowing it? Or was it just a prejudice because he seemed not quite so

fine in his nature as her beloved sister? Besides, James was prejudiced against Holt. It might be hard for him to be generous and true under those circumstances. Yet her heart rebuked her for the thought.

She stood uncertainly holding the bit of paper for a long time and finally put out the light and went and sat by the open window, trying to clear her mental vision and understand what she ought to do.

Out on the lawn the shadows were dark under the great tree where she and Jasper Holt had said good-bye. She thrilled again as she remembered.

The stars were clear and friendly as though they too remembered. The long stream of light still marked the divide between the shadows and the path to the house, for the lamps were burning brightly downstairs, though all seemed quiet. Jean had heard Eleanor come upstairs again, and tiptoe softly by her door as if fearing to wake her. She felt almost guilty, sitting there in the dark awake.

The pillows were soft in the great willow, cushioned chair she occupied, and the air was sweet that came in from the plains and sifted through the lacy shadow-work of vines. The day had been long and full of excitement, and the kindly night wrapped softly about the young sweet thing sitting with an angel's problem to decide. With the paper still held tightly in her hand, her head drooped back against the chair and she was asleep.

It might have been an hour later that she awoke, the gruff voice of a man startling her into consciousness once more.

"That you, Jim? What's the matter? It's fierce when one's having the time of his life to have to turn and run at a moment's call. What's up? Something pretty stiff or you never would have sent that message. If I find it's any nonsense and squeamishness I'll. . . ."

"Sh!"

The voice suddenly changed into a gruff whisper. Jean was sufficiently awake to realize that the man Harrington had sent for had come. Then she addressed herself to her problem again, and the voices in low mumble, gradually rising to distinguishable sentences now and then, continued under her window.

She was not conscious of hearing them until suddenly she was startled into sharp attention by a name.

"I tell you if Jasper Holt gets onto this in time it will mean state prison at least for us. It looks bad." It was Harrington's voice that spoke.

"I don't see it that way," said the stranger. "Holt hasn't got onto it, and Holt won't get onto it. You say the girl said he handed her back the wallet and never said a word. Don't you know Holt would never have let his own valuable private papers out of his hand if he had suspected in the least that she held them? You know Holt better than that. Ten to one he was so taken with the girl that he never noticed the wallet; and why would he think she had his wallet, anyway? I think it was pretty rare of old man Scathlin to think of giving the papers to her. It threw Holt entirely off the track for good. Now, what we want to do is get hold of Blount. He's the whole show up there in New York anyway. I'll just wire him to come at once and talk it over, and we'll get to work and cut off the water supply while little Jasper's training his roses and wondering what has become of his perfectly good deeds to his perfectly good silver mine."

"But one of the missing papers is the grant of water rights. If that were here we might talk. . . ."

Jean sat up suddenly with bated breath, and her arm hit against the hairbrush which, in her excitement of preparing for bed, she had laid down upon the window sill. The hairbrush fell with a sharp noise on the polished floor just over the edge of the rug, and the two men in the vine-draped porch below started fiercely and looked up, the stranger with an oath.

"What's that?"

"Oh, nothing, I guess," said Harrington, his own voice a

trifle strained. "Probably my wife has gone to tuck in the baby and dropped something. You needn't worry, my sister-in-law is fast asleep hours ago. Her light went out just after I came out here to watch for you, and there hasn't been a sound overhead since. She was worn to a frazzle."

"Where is her room. This window up here?"

"No, just next, but she's asleep, I'm sure."

Harrington rose and stepping off the porch walked out on the lawn in the edge of shadow next the path and looked up. Jean, huddled back against her great window chair, her face white with excitement, could see his attitude as he surveyed the windows and then, reassured, went back to the porch.

"It's all right," he said in a low tone, "but maybe we had better go to the other end of the porch. I was afraid of waking the baby over there, and the rascal is a difficult problem when he wakes in the night."

"Well, talk lower anyway," said the stranger. "What did you say the other missing paper was? You have the list of them all, haven't you?"

"Yes, copies. I wish we'd sent the copies instead of the originals, only Scathlin's story about finding them wouldn't have worked then. The other lost paper is the claim, with the location of the ore—*most* important. Strange that those two, the ones on which the others all hinge, are gone! I can't understand. Do you suppose Scathlin has something up his sleeve? Maybe he kept only those two and means to get these later. But what object could he have had?"

There was silence for a moment while the two men thought.

At last Garrett spoke: "What do you suppose Holt was doing on that train—the same train with Scathlin? Holt didn't leave home till Scathlin had been on his way nearly two days. When was the last we heard from Scathlin?"

"Pittsburgh. A telegram. He'd just arrived," answered Harrington glumly.

"What day was that? Could Holt have reached Pittsburgh

before Scathlin got away? He's sharp you know. Have you got the telegram?"

"It's inside," said Harrington. "Just step in." And the two men went into the house. Jean could hear their low, troubled voices, rumbling on, but she could not hear any more words, and she sat shivering over what she had heard.

Scathlin! Scathlin! Why was that word so familiar? Scathlin! Ah! She had heard it from the lips of Holt himself, before she went into the sleeper. It was what he had called the old man.

Was this wrong, this involuntary eavesdropping? She had not meant to listen, had never thought there might be anything said that she would understand, or that they would care if she did hear, until the whole revelation was in her possession; and then she was too much frightened to stir or think what she ought to do. Was it not right, perhaps, that she should have heard; and, yet, what could she do? It was all too evident that Jasper Holt was about to be cheated in some way. That remark about his private papers was unmistakable. And the little paper in her hand that had to do with water rights was his also. Water rights were sacred things in the west, and most important. The losing of them had often been the cause of the sweeping away of whole fortunes she knew; and the little bit of paper that proved his right was in her trembling hand to bestow where she would! It was plain that if she should go down now and give it to those two men she would be most welcome; but she was sure that it would not be right for them to have it. They had admitted enough to make her feel that there was some plot against Holt; and suddenly all her latent dislike of her brother-in-law, which had been lying dormant through the years because there was nothing to rouse it, sprang into being. Her decision was made. She must somehow get that paper to Jasper Holt, and that just as soon as possible. She must not let her brother-in-law know that she had it. If she were mistaken about this, Jasper Holt would be true and tell her so and return the paper. She felt as sure of him as if she had known him all her life. But there *could* be no mistake. It *must* be his. The men had practically admitted it!

It made her shiver with cold to think how dreadful all this was. Brought up to strictest integrity, it seemed terrible that one in her own family should swerve from it; there must be some other explanation to the talk she had heard. Things in the business world were often hard to understand, and a lot of shady things were done under the name of righteousness. She had heard her father talk about "graft"; maybe it was something like that. Maybe James thought he was doing good service to cut Jasper Holt out of his water rights somehow; and maybe, in some strange unexplainable way, he was justified. And yet . . . what did they mean about the location of the silver mine? Oh, it was too much for her! If she had never known and loved Jasper Holt, and trusted him, she would have gone down and put the whole thing in James's hands and gone to bed thinking nothing further about it. But now her whole soul was roused to do the right thing toward her rescuer, who, she saw, was under the ban, and who seemed to her to be in the right in this case at least.

It occurred to her how easily she might wash her hands of the whole matter by dropping that bit of paper out of her window and letting it be found or not, as the case might be. How easy to live sometimes if one had no conscience to reckon with—and no heart!

It seemed a long time that she sat trembling by the open window, afraid to stir lest the men downstairs should hear her move; unable to think connectedly and decide what she ought to do. But at last the two men came out on the piazza again, the guest apparently about to take his leave. His voice had lost its easy assurance.

"It looks bad!" he said, "very bad! It looks as if Scathlin has bungled things. If Holt suspects we have anything to do with it, why, our fish is dished. I guess there's nothing else to do but send him back those papers, saying that a stranger put them into your sister-in-law's hands to bring to you, and you know nothing about them, but seeing his name among them you suppose they must be his. You could add a word about being grateful for his care of the girl or something of the sort to make it look natural."

"But that throws all the responsibility on me," said Harrington angrily. "And it looks mighty funny to have those two important papers gone. These are no use to anybody without the others."

"Of course, but you're not supposed to know that, and he can't do anything but bluster. Anyhow, as far as I see, it's your only chance, and you'll have to do it mighty quick or that won't do any good. I wouldn't keep them a day...."

"I shall do nothing of the kind," snarled Harrington. "I would rather destroy them than play into his hand that way. I'm not in a position to throw suspicion on myself in that style."

"Do as you please," said the guest scornfully. "That's my advice. I wash my hands of it. If you want to hang on to a lost cause for the sake of pride you'll have to do it without me. I know when to quit."

"But suppose Scathlin returns in a few days with Blount."

"Scathlin won't return with Blount. You can take my word for that. Either Scathlin's dead or he's sold those other two papers to Holt and given away our secrets into the bargain. You may depend on it. If Scathlin was all right he'd have telegraphed at intervals as he was ordered. There's some reason why he quit telegraphing at Pittsburgh."

Garrett departed noisily, and after a few minutes pacing up and down the piazza Harrington went in, put out the lights and went upstairs.

Jean crept softly into bed, still grasping the paper close to her heart; and weary, troubled, bewildered she soon fell fast asleep.

Later, when the moon had died and only the luminous mist in the east proclaimed the dawn at hand, a rider came quietly down the road, his horse stepping as if with padded feet, and stopped before the house.

The rider dismounted silently in the darkness and with noiseless tread came and laid something down in the dewy silence at the door. Then he mounted and slipped away into the darkness again.

Chapter 10

Down the long, silent road beyond the sleeping town the rider passed, out to the plains. His horse knew the trail well, was rested and glad to be used. He stepped away into the gray dawning carrying his beloved master with willing feet. There was no need to hurry him. He seemed to know as if by instinct just how fast to travel to arrive at the Junction in time for the early morning train. It was not the first time he had journeyed thus at that hour.

The rider sat upon his horse as one who had begun a long quest which might not end this side the other world. There was weariness in his attitude, and profound thoughtfulness, with steady determination to pursue his way to the end.

Now and then he bent his head and laid his lips on the cool fragrance of a great, dim bud stuck carelessly into his buttonhole, its branch and thorns and leaves still attached as if it might have been plucked from the vine by hasty impulse. Later, when the day came up and houses were in sight, he tore it from its stem and wrapped it quickly in his handkerchief to hide away in his pocket.

The stars were paling when he started. They slipped one by one silently into the oblivion of a background of light as he rode, but before they left him they spoke many things to his sad, determined soul. Sometimes it almost seemed to him that a girl rode at his side and understood his thoughts.

His thoughts were as one would go with lighted lamp and eyes suddenly awake to see, through the long, unvisited chambers of his soul, and find with startled senses the dirt and cobwebs and musty, dusty corners, cluttered with moth-eaten garments of a dead past; and, searching closer in dark crannies, find the bones of dead things that should have lived but for the unwatchful keeper of that house.

The young face lost its boyishness and grew grave and haggard with suffering. Then he laid his lips on the cool flower petals and heard again the voice of the girl like music in his soul: "I will trust you always, no matter what anybody says!" and it thrilled him and gave him courage, so that when morning burst upon the plain and he came in sight of the straggling houses surrounding the Junction, he lifted up his face to the golden morning sky and breathed aloud solemnly.

"Oh God! Help me to keep my vow to her, always, even to the end of life! Help me to be what she believes me to be! Help me to be worthy of her trust!"

With these words upon his lips and the memory of her kiss upon his brow he went forward into the new day and the new life that was before him. This duty that was his today was by no means a pleasant one, and it might be long and hard, but he must do it in a way different from that which he would have done three days before, for today he was a different creature. He had seen himself as he was before God, and henceforth all things were become new.

He was in time to make all his arrangements to leave the horse before the train arrived. He had chosen to travel across country to the Junction rather than to take the train at his home station, partly to avoid publicity, and partly to save time, for there was no train from Hawk Valley early enough to connect with this eastern express which stopped at the Junction. Passengers from Hawk Valley wishing to catch this train would be forced to leave the evening before and put up at the Junction tavern, a most unpleasant experience for any traveler. Jasper Holt preferred traveling on horseback at all times to riding on the railroad; and besides, every minute counted now in the errand he was on his way to perform.

All the morning while the train glided over the level plain
he was going over his recent experience; going back to the
moment when the girl entered upon his vision and looked at
him with that clear, direct gaze that trusted him; thinking
over every detail of his finding her in the darkness and peril;
the miracle that he and not some other should have found
and saved her; recalling every incident of the beautiful,
wearisome way by which they had gone home together; and
the wonder of the girl's faith in him, her love for him—his
love for her.

Anyone watching the absorbed, silent man sitting alone,
his head dropped back against the seat, his hat drawn down
over his eyes, the lines of gravity deep upon brow and lip
and chin, would have judged him for a much older man
than he was, so maturing had life thus far been to him.

And now, the task that was before him was to find Scathlin—if, indeed, he were still in the land of the living—or
some evidence that he was dead; and to know beyond a
question of doubt what had become of those papers, and just
how far Harrington had been responsible for the theft.

He loathed his task, yet felt compelled by some inner urg-
ing to finish it. Almost his soul revolted to the extent of giving up the case and letting his enemies triumph over him.
What to him now was his silver mine, since he had found
her—and lost her forever? Why not let his property go and
leave Hawk Valley forever, where his reputation had undone him in his greatest opportunity? Why not go to some
new land where he was unknown and begin all over again?

But his soul was too strong and true for that. He must face
his mistakes in the place where he had made them and
undo, if might be, some of the harm he had done. He had to
do this whether he would or no. It was right that he should
find his papers and make good his claim. It was a part of the
true living he had set himself from this time forth. He had
promised to let people see that he was trustworthy and this
was the first step. If Harrington and his men got their way he

would be branded as a thief and a liar again and the old reputation only fixed the firmer.

It was toward evening when they passed the scene of the late disaster and the long rays of the sun rested over the river and the valley where peril and death had brooded. A temporary way had been made for the tracks, all signs of death and disaster swept hastily out of sight by the wrecking train, and the tide of travel was already rolling calmly on again. A swarm of workmen, like ants carrying grains of sand over a wall, were at work on the broken bridge, and the passing traveler looked cheerfully across and got no hint of fire and fear and sudden death. Even the trainmen had had their orders and answered gruffly, in brief sentences, when questioned about the wreck, turning it off lightly as a small thing, until they heard that here was one of the victims of the accident. Then they looked sharply a second time and stole back to talk in low tones with guarded sentences about where the blame should lie. But no one knew much about the details, after all. The conductor reluctantly admitted that the victims, those who had been saved, had been taken to the nearest city and distributed among the hospitals. That was all. He implied that there were many victims who had not even that comfort.

So, to the nearest city went Jasper Holt, arriving shortly after sundown, to begin his search among the hospitals at once, after having visited the railroad office and gotten all the information they could give him.

Three days and two nights Jasper Holt searched, in hospitals and morgue, and even private homes. Wherever he could learn of a person who had been through the accident he went to see if they knew any clue to the man he sought, but not a hint did he find.

It was entirely reasonable to suppose that Scathlin had lost his life in the fire or the river, and to feel that further search was unnecessary. But Jasper Holt, standing at the window of his hotel room and looking out on the busy streets of that western city toward evening of the third day, could not feel it so. More and more it became necessary to find that man, or be sure of his death. The three days of visiting hospitals and viewing suffering and death had graven the sad lines even deeper in his fine, strong face. It began to seem now to him that he might even have a *duty* toward that loathsome creature Scathlin, though heaven knows why any such thought should have entered his head, seeing he was the injured, not the injuring. But the more he thought about it the more he felt that he must search further.

To look any longer in the city was absurd. He had already covered every clue that he had found, and the railroad authorities were beginning to grow weary of this assiduous young man with the firm jaw and the blue-gray eyes of steel who steadily demanded the missing man. They offered to send him back to the scene of the accident with a man to help him, and authority to get assistance from their workmen to search the river and vicinity. This offer Jasper finally accepted and the next morning was on his way back.

The last time Holt had seen Scathlin he had not really seen him at all, he had merely sensed his presence in the darkness.

They had both been sleeping—Scathlin with the relaxation of one who no longer needs to be on the alert, Holt with half his senses on guard—when the crash came. Splintering glass and a rush of cold air brought Holt clearly to himself. The car had been turned on end and was sinking, sinking down with creak and groan; and the two men were thrown together for a moment into the aisle, clinging to the arms of the seats. Holt had heard the terrible oaths with which Scathlin was wont to embroider his speech even on calmer occasions. They sounded now like a challenge to the Almighty. The younger man had reached out a hand in the darkness to strike the other, and had uttered a single sentence, "Cut that out!" but the profanity continued, and Scathlin had struck him a blow blindly across his eyes which bewildered him for a second and made the confusion more black and terrible. Then he had been aware that Scathlin was scrambling up over the arm of the seat to the window, and was climbing out. The red glow from outside flared up and showed Scathlin's bulk against the night, his head and shoulders already out the window, the stream of oaths not so distinct now because they were flung to the outdoor world.

It was then that he realized that Scathlin was escaping from him and he must not let him get away. Even in such a situation he remembered his long quest, and pulling himself up by main force, caught Scathlin by the foot. Suddenly he remembered the curious actions of Scathlin the day before, and his fumbling with his shoestrings afterwards. The shoe Holt held in his firm grip was laced and tied in a hard knot, but Holt's knife was ready and he cut the string in several places. Scathlin did not stay for shoes. He left his footgear readily in his pursuer's hands and made good his escape, but Holt, forgetful of his peril for the moment, searched in the shoe and found a folded paper.

It was too dark to tell if the paper were one of those he sought. He put it safely in his pocket for further investigation, felt in the shoe carefully once more to make sure there was not another, and then climbed out of the window after Scathlin. But when he dropped into the melee below he could not see Scathlin anywhere. There were some rocks far below, and down there he had thought he saw a white face as he first looked from the window before he leaped, when the fire broke out with a flare. But after he had dropped and found himself in the water he could not quite locate the rocks again, and while he was searching he saw another victim drop and sink and rise again and he went to her rescue. So had Scathlin had his wish and escaped from the train before they reached the region of Hawk Valley?

Holt and his assistant searched the scene of the wreck until the young man was convinced that further search was useless, and sent the man back to the city. Then he dropped down to the river bank and talked with one or two men on the wrecking crew while they were waiting for the construction train to come and bear them back to their camp, and here for the first time he got a clue. They had found a man down on the rocks with a broken leg a whole day after the others had been taken to the city hospital. Some bushes had hid him and no one had noticed him till they heard him groaning and cursing. A man who said he had a shack "up a piece" had taken him in his wagon. He had promised to get a doctor and fix the man up. The man himself had begged them to shoot him. He was almost out of his head with suffering. Their vague description tallied with Scathlin's rough appearance and Holt became convinced he had found his man.

Making the best he could out of their indefinite directions, for they really had not much idea of the locality of that shack themselves, Holt started off in search.

He found Scathlin before nightfall that same day, lying alone and moaning with pain and fever in the deserted shack. The householder had gone away at dawn on business, promising a speedy return, but had not come back, and Scathlin, his broken bone set rudely by an unskilled hand, lay suffering. When Holt pushed the door open and looked in he started up with a yell, his eyes protruding in fear. He thought that Holt was dead in the fire of the wreck, and this was his spirit come to demand account.

It was only when Holt laid his cool hand on the dirty, crusted brow and spoke in his quiet voice of command, that Scathlin settled back, the terror still in his eyes, and consented to be still. He began gradually to realize that Holt was there in the flesh, and that not for retribution either. He had not succeeded in escaping his captor. He never could do that. But his captor would not be a tormentor. That was plain. He had heard that Holt was "square" with his men, but had never believed it. Now he had opportunity to judge for himself. And so cunning and contemptible was the creature that when he was once assured of the fact that Holt would not strike him when he was down, he at once set about to take advantage of it. It was as if he had found a spot of honor wherein Holt was vulnerable, and there, upon his bed of pain, in his loathsome helplessness, with no one to relieve him but Holt, he attacked that one pregnable spot of Holt's fortress. Day and night he moaned and fretted. Hour after hour he demanded this and that, whining like a baby and cursing like a demon by turns.

The householder did not return. It is possible that something ill befell him in that lonely plain over which he journeyed skirting the desert; it is probable that he had had enough of Scathlin's complaints and was glad to escape from his unwelcome guest. However it was, Holt was there alone with him for many days, nursing him as tenderly as a woman might have done; bearing with his varying moods; washing him, feeding him, cooling his hot forehead. Only once did Scathlin lapse from his role of pampered patient and beg with terror and abject humility in his eyes and voice, and that was the day when Holt declared his intention of going after a doctor. Scathlin was sure that Holt meant to desert him, and he cried like a baby, swore like a mad man, and then pleaded and promised contritely. But it was all to no avail and Holt left him for a few hours, with a supply at hand for every need, and went for a doctor. Scathlin's cries and curses followed him as far as he could hear, and something like pity came into his heart for the poor, wicked old criminal, so that he hastened his steps with all his might.

When he returned four hours later with a gruff but kindly doctor, the cunning look came back into the little beady eyes, and the bristly old jaw grew stubborn and selfish again. He saw that Holt's honor still held and he meant to get the worth of his money out of him.

The doctor came every few days after that and Scathlin improved rapidly, growing more arrogant every day.

Holt went about silently for the most part; nursing the

patient, cooking his meals—there were a few supplies in the shack and Holt had bought more when he went for the doctor—and there was game to be had for the shooting. There was something about his set, stern face even in his gentleness that sometimes shamed Scathlin and silenced him for a while. It was as if his mind was far away on higher things, and Scathlin's petty torments did not reach up into the rarefied air where he really lived.

Once when he was getting better and sitting up Scathlin attempted a story, so vile and low that the devil himself must have originated it. He laughed immoderately as he told it, hoping to break the stern sadness of Holt's face, which fairly made him frantic to look at, but Holt looked at him with a kind of pity for a second, and then the sternness grew terrible.

"Scathlin, cut that out, you beast!" he said, and left the cabin for the open air. It was that day that Holt had a struggle with himself to stick to his job.

There was no longer the necessity that brought him. The papers, the rest of them, wherever they were, were surely not here. Holt had gone over every inch of Scathlin's clothes and possessions, and there was no place where he could possibly have hid them about the shack that Holt had not looked. He had watched Scathlin by night and day when he did not know he was being watched, and he was convinced that Scathlin was no longer protecting any papers of his. The one which he had taken from the toe of Scathlin's shoe had proved to be his own and most important. What Scathlin had done with the rest he was not sure, but it was probable that he had given some of them to Jean with the wallet which he had, of course, recognized, when he picked it up and handed it to her. It was also possible that the man who owned the shack had, by some means, been wheedled into taking the papers back to Harrington. Every circumstance made his speedy return to Hawk Valley advisable, and yet here he was chained to this helpless, peevish old man, who when he was done with him, would, if he could, stab him in the back for all he had done for him.

If anything of all this passed through Jasper Holt's mind as he paced up and down alone outside the cabin, he kept it to himself, and it made no mark upon his face. Just as patiently and just as kindly he waited on that ungrateful old creature, all the time seeming to live himself on a higher plane and breathe a higher air; and the old man hated him for it.

And so as the days at last came when the patient could walk about a little, the beady old eyes took on new cunning, the grizzly jaw grew more set, the whining complaints became more pitiful; and when Holt urged that now the time had come when they might go home without harm to the mending limb, Scathlin's eyes filled with fear, and he whined and begged for just a little longer. For once more the vision of the stark tree against the sky, the swinging body, the retreating backs of Holt's strong men, haunted Scathlin's memory; and his terror returned with each day of his recovery.

One day when Holt had gone at last to a settlement to procure a wagon and some other necessities for the journey, he returned to find the cunning old ingrate gone!

At first it seemed only a relief from a disagreeable task, and he would have let him go, only again there seemed that inner sense of finishing a task which made him go out and search. For he knew the weak leg could not carry the man far, and he felt too that he must keep hold of Scathlin and take him back to face what he should find awaiting him in Hawk Valley of good or ill. He might need the old man for a witness.

And so he drew him from his crouching shelter, spoke to him firmly, and made a compact with him, for he recognized his fear. That night saw the two again on their way to Hawk

Valley. Scathlin was to have shelter and food, and work when he was able, but in return he must abide by certain rules. Scathlin, relieved and cunning still, promised eagerly, with many mental reservations; and so the pilgrimage at last was ended, and Holt was going back—back where the girl he loved was staying—the girl he loved, but might not see!

Chapter 11

There had been no fuss made over Jasper Holt when he was born. They handed him an honored name from some fierce old warrior of a forebear, relegated him to a fourth-story back nursery with a trained nurse, and left him to himself.

His mother paused long enough before returning to her interrupted social career to look him over, declare that he had nice eyes and she believed his hair was going to curl; then she was swallowed up in the world from which she had reluctantly stepped aside. She had little use for a son except to dress him in velvets and Lord Fauntleroy collars and make of him a toy to amuse her guests. Until he reached that stage she saw very little of him.

Of his stern father he saw less. He was immersed in business. He was rich, but what of that? He had to make more riches to keep the social whirl fed.

The baby had a face and form worth noticing, even in his first days. The great blue eyes that had attracted his mother's flitting attention, could be gray sometimes, and had in them depths of light and wisdom that fairly startled his practical nurse. He had the brow of a philosopher, and gold hair rippled around the fine little head like a halo. The old warrior-namesake must have bestowed upon him that firm chin beneath the cupid's bow of the lips, and surely an angel had lent him that smile!

But as he grew older there came into his eyes a wistfulness that was almost pathetic at times. He was an affectionate child, quite embarrassing his cold, reserved nurse with his demonstrations, but winning the utmost devotion always from all who had to serve him.

He was not a good boy in the conventional meaning of the word. He sweetly and serenely had his own way in everything from the time he could walk and talk. He would neither eat what he did not like, nor wear what he did not fancy. He did not take kindly to his mother's velvets and curls and lace collars. He always disappeared hopelessly when made ready for a dress parade. He would fight any bully on the back street who undertook to cheat the little lame newsboy, and he was always trying to take the part of some weak dog or child. He could run down the street with the swiftness of a swallow, his pockets full of sharp stones, and hit every electric light in the block as he ran, and he was forever taking the blame frankly for all the broken windows and looted garden plots in the neighborhood. In these days his acquaintance with his father was limited to severe interviews in which stern threats and scathing reprimands mingled with galling sarcasm. It was as his clear eyes looked steadily, unafraidly, into the angry steel ones of his father that his young face hardened; his warrior chin took a firm set, and the light in his face was deadened by a stab of pain. He was growing wise and losing his faith in the love he had taken for granted in both father and mother. It was at that time that he lived mostly upon the street, and companioned with boys of the rougher class. No one but his nurse knew it, and she but seldom. She was only too glad to have the time off duty.

It was when they discovered a childish plot in the neighborhood to mob the president of a defaulting bank in which the hardworking parents of some of his playmates had lost their all, that Jasper was taken hold of by the law as leader and financier of the whole enterprise. Bravely, proudly, he took the whole blame, exonerating the other boys, and declaring himself instigator of the affair.

His father paid a heavy fine to hush it up and took his son in charge. A merciless whipping was the beginning of that interview between them, which the son received like a gentleman. But when it was over he lifted reproachful eyes, steadied his quivering warrior chin and said determinedly: "But all the same, Father, I think I *was right!* That man had been *stealing* those poor people's money!"

The father looked at the little son with the unbroken will and *swore!* He took away the cheap little firearms that the boy had purchased with his allowance for himself and the other boys, and he declared the allowance should cease until such time as the boy would own to his fault and come to his senses. One isn't just quite sure, but, perhaps after all, the removal of his allowance was the very best thing that the father ever did for his little, lonely son who had begun so early to reform the world with a high hand.

Jasper went up to his room and thought. Then he went out and consulted with a newsboy friend of his, and presently he was established on a paper route of his own. For several weeks he sold papers till he had enough money to replace his lost revolver. Then he was satisfied and retired from business for a time. But this was not his first business venture, and his father began to discover that the threat of taking away the allowance had no effect whatever on his determined young son.

Yet, in spite of his bravery and strength, in spite of his high purposes and anarchistic tendencies, there was in the boy's nature a great wealth of love and a desire to be loved. He was, in his younger days, forever throwing his arms about his beautiful mother's neck and kissing her to her great disgust and the severe detriment of her complexion; until finally he became shy about showing his affection, and the lines of loneliness and yearning grew deeper about the young mouth.

It was the time he ran away that made him sure that no one cared for him.

Jasper had been up before the paternal tribunal for some trivial offense, and his word had not been taken in explanation, against the word of his younger brother—who had arrived on the scene some three years later than himself, and through some strange fantasy of selfishness was the beloved darling of his mother.

Perry Holt had sharp little effeminate features like his mother's, and had been petted and spoiled from the moment his whimsical mother first saw him. If there was any trouble Perry was usually at the bottom of it and Jasper was blamed for it, because Jasper was "so fresh" and "so wild" and "always getting into trouble and doing what he ought not to do." That was the way his mother put it. And so she had ordered Jasper to his father's den for a reprimand for something Perry really had done, and Jasper's word was doubted!

He took his punishment silently and went to his room and his bed, where he lay motionless staring into the darkness. If he had been a girl he might have sobbed, so hurt was his soul; but being Jasper he held back the stinging tears that burned his eyes and stared hard into the dark. At midnight, when the servants were asleep, he arose and stole softly from the house before his mother and father had returned from some social function they were attending.

He stayed away three days, companioning with waifs who had no homes, and then his homesick heart brought him back again with longing to see his mother. He reached the house at early dusk and found his mother and Perry getting into the car to ride to the station where they were to meet his father and take a pleasure trip to Washington for a few days! They had not even missed him and were going off without knowing where he was! His mother looked at him with disgust and told him to go into the house and wash his face, that he "looked a perfect fright," and then the car whirled off and left him gazing after his dream of what a mother ought to be.

After that Jasper never expected anything more from his mother or his family. He began to see that life was meant to be a lonely job and it "was up to him" how it turned out. He seemed to grow up and be wise beyond his years in those few seconds that he stood gazing after the car vanishing in the dusk.

When it was discovered that he was spending most of his time on the street in the company of newsboys and working-men's sons, he was fitted out expensively and sent away to boarding school where he began a lively career. Those who understood him adored him, but they were few, and were mostly confined to small boys and the working class. The little boys in the school followed him like flies after molasses and obeyed him abjectly. The teachers dreaded and feared and hated him almost to a man, with the exception of now and then a woman who had an unusual amount of fine instinct and saw the yearning for love in his eyes.

From school to school he went, out of one scrape into another, yet no one stopped to inquire what it was all about or to discover that almost every trouble he got into was for the sake of someone else, or some real principle. That his efforts at reform were against the rules of the school and could therefore but fail, made no difference to him. He went right on setting things right as far as he could and then taking the consequences. He saw the futility of his efforts and sometimes clenched his sturdy fists and thought of the future when he should be able to "lick" those unfair teachers who couldn't see that they were letting some fellows go scot-free who were more to blame than the ones who were punished. Someday he would be bigger than they, and then he would back up his protests with a strength that could not be gainsaid. And so he went on fighting bullies who were bigger than himself and who did not hesitate to put the whole story in a good light for themselves; and taking the consequences in such a way that when he left a school the principal had beneath his open relief a troubled undertone of smallness, and of feeling that, after all, the boy had got the better of him, for there had been the look of a conqueror in Jasper's eye as he parted from him at the station.

Somehow he got himself through with his preparatory studies and was allowed to pass on. It surely was not from any great scholastic attainments, for he never bothered himself to learn lessons that he did not care for, nor to recite them after he had learned them, and examinations meant nothing at all to him. If he chose to take one he did so, and then spoiled the whole paper by some erratic tirade of his own on some special question; or else took the whole thing as a joke. If he did not choose to take an examination he calmly sat through the allotted time intent upon his own thoughts and handed in no paper at the close. His teachers raved and ranted. They punished and they threatened. But Jasper went calmly on and did as he pleased; and strange to say in all that checkered career there were but two teachers who understood the soul with whom they had to deal, and could lead him like a lamb by a mere smile or word to do the hardest tasks. For those two he slaved, not because he saw any reason in their demands always, but because he desired to please them, for they had proved themselves what he called "square."

Nevertheless he had acquired through it all a most marvelous and varied amount of knowledge. Nothing escaped him. He never forgot anything he heard, and the classes through which he had sat, perpetrating many of his jokes upon the teachers, had all left their impress upon him. What he had heard the other students recite, that he knew. If you began to quote a line of poetry which had been studied in English class he would promptly finish it and, when he chose, tell you much about the author. His teachers would have been amazed if they could have heard him. And often when another fellow took a high rank in the class in mathematics it had been Jasper who had showed him how to work his problems—problems that he had not taken the trouble to work out for himself.

"Why should I?" he once answered a troublesome principal who was admonishing him about preparing his lessons.

"I get what I need out of them, and that's all that's necessary, isn't it? It's *my* education, isn't it? My teacher isn't getting any good out of my writing out all that junk, is he? It isn't doing *him* any good, why should I take the trouble?"

And this was his hopeless attitude whenever he had to deal with teachers whom he did not reverence.

In college he was much the same, only that it did not matter there so much. There were more men and he was less under authority. It was expected that he should have some independence. Yet even here he was mixed up in a great many troubles. Finally, in his third year, his college career came to a sudden and final ending in the midst of a disgrace that was not his own, but which he took upon his own sturdy shoulders to save another youth who had a widowed mother dependent upon him, and must get through college before he could support her. Whether or not his action was justified by the following chapters of that weak and careless youth's life is not a part of this story to tell. It may be that Jasper himself learned some lessons by the disgrace he took upon himself and the lightness with which the real criminal accepted his sacrifice. However that may be, Jasper's mother, by that time an attractive widow, was so thoroughly outraged by her son's behavior—she never knew, of course, that he himself had not been at fault—that she drove him from his home in scorn and contempt.

Hurt to the heart the boy obeyed; too proud to explain; knowing she would be but the angrier if she knew the truth; knowing there was no mother heart in her for him, nor ever had been.

He went straight to the great, wide free west, and roamed for a year from one place to another restlessly, still expecting someday to return when his mother should feel differently. Then he saw in the papers the notice of her marriage to a man he never had liked, and so he settled down on the claim he had already taken, and built up around his young, lonely life a something which he called home.

Gradually the outcasts of society had been drawn to him for help or comfort in dire need and peril from the law; and always he had sympathy with any who were without the pale of the respectable world, even though in no other way could he feel anything congenial about them. His home came to be the refuge for sinners, and because their crimes were many and his hearth was wide, their sins were fastened to him in name if not in deed; as when a child he bore the blame for others and himself grew strong.

He built them rude dwellings on his land, and some he chose to be his trusted ones. One by one he tested them and found them true to him and to his few simple principles of life. Sternly he ruled them, and greatly did they love and reverence their boy leader, and were proud to follow him. If one of them transgressed again he was dealt with justly; and once a body swayed and hung stark against the sky in justice for a deed of shame. It was this memory that Scathlin held and feared, although it had happened long before he came to take refuge from some petty deed of his. Scathlin had never entered the closer brotherhood of men who guarded Holt's own private quarters. His place had been upon the outer edge of things. He was not trusted—never had been—and knew he was not trustworthy. So it was that he dreaded going back to those relentless men, who, if they once found out that he had robbed their leader of valuable property and betrayed him into the hands of an enemy who had long looked with hungry eyes at the rich silver mine and abundant water supply that were his, would stop at nothing till justice had been done upon his contemptible head. But by that same honor that made men love and serve him, old Scathlin knew that Holt had not yet told his men about his loss of the wallet, nor whom he suspected.

This was Jasper Holt, and this his story up to the time that he met Jean and laid his roses at her threshold.

Chapter 12

It was late when Jean awoke. The household had been quiet on her account, and breakfast was delayed. Jean came down white with her vigil, but sweet and smiling notwithstanding.

The morning had brought clear vision and she was sure now that the paper in her possession must be given to Holt and no other. She had settled so much and would await her opportunity. This decided, her mind was at peace, and she entered the dining room with a smile of greeting for everyone.

Late as it was, the master of the house had not yet appeared and the family stood about waiting for him. But as Jean entered the servant came in from an opposite door with his arms full of roses, and stood before her.

Such roses! Jean had never seen such wealth of beauty, such luxuriance of coloring. They all exclaimed in wonder over them! Clear, golden yellow with a deep, rosy tint at heart like liquid rubies spilled into them. Great heavy-headed buds and full-blown roses in abundance, many of them still on the trailing vines, as if they had been plucked with ruthless hand to offer to a queen; their fragrance filled the room like a burst of incense from some oriental shrine. The servant laid them in her arms as though he were offering her a crown and scepter.

"How wonderful!" murmured the girl, receiving them and laying her face reverently down to their exquisite beauty. "Where did they come from? Are they mine? Do they grow here?"

"I found them at the door, Miss," said the man respectfully. "There's only a card with your name."

"Why, how strange!" said Mrs. Harrington, stepping forward to inspect the card. "Who could have sent them? I have told a number of the young men about your coming, and they are all eager to see you; but it's strange that whoever sent these beautiful roses shouldn't have given his name. They are wonderfully rare. Somebody must have squandered his month's earnings on them. They couldn't have been bought around here. I suppose they came from some florist a long way off."

The discreet servant narrowed his eyes and turned away suddenly as he saw his master enter.

"Just look here, James, what beautiful roses someone has sent Jean! Wasn't that lovely of him, whoever he is? They were at the door when John opened it this morning, and no name on them! Who do you suppose could have sent them? Stockton Holmes, or Gartney Fowler, or even Captain Wetherill, perhaps?"

But the master of the house glanced sharply at the roses and a frown came between his brows.

"There's only one place around here where roses like that grow," he announced ominously.

His wife looked at him with a frightened expression.

"You don't mean. . . ."

"Yes," said Harrington. "They're Holt's Golden Sunset!"

There was an ominous silence as the husband and wife looked at each other. Then Mrs. Harrington turned to her sister, who stood behind her roses with an exquisite flush on her cheeks and a soft, burning light of battle in her eyes.

"Jean, did you know where they came from?" her sister asked, almost haughtily.

But Jean's lovely face showed no sign of intimidation as she raised it, gravely sweet, from the roses which she held as she might have held a little child.

"I thought perhaps Mr. Holt sent them," she said simply. "He told me about his roses. But excuse me just a minute till I put them in water. I won't keep you waiting."

When Jean returned after laying her roses tenderly in the washbowl in her room and bending to touch her lips to their petals, there was no look on her face as if anything unusual had passed except a kind of glorified light in her eyes. She began at once to give her sister a message from their mother, tactfully ignoring the flowers and their donor. But Harrington's set look did not relax during the entire meal.

After breakfast there was the whole place to be seen; the garden, the horses, the rabbits, and the new tennis court, the only one in town, where the young officers from the fort came down to play sometimes.

The children came out of their shyness and adopted their new relative ecstatically, monopolizingly. They drew her down on the garden seat and plied her with questions, and they chattered away happily, feeling her hair, touching her cheek softly now and then, playing with the ribbons at her throat.

"Papa's awfully angry that Jasper Holt brought you home," confided Betty. "I heard him tell Mamma he'd rather have lost fifty thousand dollars than had it happen."

The color stole into Jean's cheeks and a flash came in her eyes, but she tried to control herself. She did not want to discuss this matter with the children, and yet she felt that she must be true to the man who had saved her life.

"Mr. Holt was very kind to me, Betty," she said quietly. "I'm sorry he is not a friend of your papa's. If he hadn't taken care of me I would probably have drowned, and I'm sure I never would have got safely here. He was wonderful!"

"Jasper Holt's a bad, wicked man," said Jamie, looking at her with round eyes and a frown that was a very good imitation of his father's. "He-he-he *hanged* a man once! On a *tree!* Yes, he *did!* Tied a string around his neck and hung him up hard till he died! He's a *nawful* bad man. Nicky Deens told me that. My mamma don't know he told me. Nicky said not to tell. But Nicky Deens saw the tree once when he went with his papa out to the desert riding, and he heard the men tell all about it. They didn't know he heard it, but he *did*."

"I don't think much of a little boy that tells you not to tell your mother things," said Jean in a choking voice. "I don't believe I shall like Nicky Deens."

"Oh, you will," said Jamie in distress for his friend. "He's a *nawful* nice boy. He can ride a horse just like his papa." Jamie launched into a description of the prowess of Nicky Deens, but Jean, although she tried to smile, was not listening. Her heart was in a tumult and her eyes were full of fire and indignation. Jasper had told her about that man who hung on the tree. She knew the whole story with all its circumstances, and she knew that Nicky Deens had heard a false account of the affair. Suddenly she turned on her astonished young nephew and spoke.

"Jamie," she said looking earnestly into his big, blue eyes, "Jamie, I want to tell you something. That story you heard about Mr. Holt is not true. He is not a bad man. People don't know. He is good and kind, and he has been Auntie Jean's friend. It isn't right nor fair for you to listen to stories about him. Little boys like Nicky Deens don't know about things always, and maybe they don't mean to tell what isn't true, but if you love Auntie Jean and believe she tells you what is true you will not let anybody say bad things anymore about Mr. Holt. It isn't necessary for you to talk about it at all if your papa doesn't like Mr. Holt, but you don't need to listen to unpleasant things about him. People have not understood Mr. Holt, or they would not have talked that way."

Jamie looked at her with round, wondering eyes, and his paternal frown grew. He did not like to have his thrilling story spoiled by being told it was not true, but then, this new aunt had pretty eyes and a smile that was good. Besides, she had promised to tell him a story, so, with mental reservations, he said, "Aw right, I won't!" and sighed to relinquish this choice bit of gossip, even during the period of his aunt's stay.

It was a relief to Jean that her sister came just then and sent the children off to play, sitting down for a real visit about home and their dear ones.

Finally there came a pause in their conversation about home and the two sisters looked at each other contentedly, glad to be together again after the long separation.

"Jean, dear," said Eleanor eagerly, "I hope you're going to have a lovely time while you're here. I've told every man in the region about you and they are dying to call on you. I don't know how many have tried to bribe me to let them be first. There is no end of charming young fellows here. The post being so near brings some of them, you know, and they love to come over to our house and get a real home meal and a glimpse of something like what they are used to. There's Charlie Evans, you'll like him I know. He's quite serious, thought of studying for the ministry at one time, but I understand he began to be rather skeptical and gave it up. You'll be just the one to do a little missionary work on him. You have great talents in that direction I remember. Mother has been telling me what wonders you've worked in your Sunday school class at the mission. And there's Freeman Thorne, he's grave and serious enough to suit your most solemn mood; and there are scores of others. You'll have flowers and invitations, more than you can attend to, pretty soon. We've lots of plans made already to help you have a good time. But I want to give you a little warning, dear." A kind of constraint came in her voice. "Don't speak about Jasper Holt unless you have to, and then the very briefest word. He isn't in good repute at all, indeed, he isn't! I understand how grateful you feel, of course; you weren't in a position to judge what kind of a fellow he was. I don't suppose one's manners would show up very badly in the woods when two people had been drowning and barely escaped with their lives. People don't think of manners at such a time."

"Eleanor, he was a perfect gentleman," put in Jean indignantly. "There were lots of chances to show unrefinement, and he was a *perfect gentleman* every time. You don't understand, Eleanor."

"Well, now dear, you'll have to trust me a little. I know just what he is, *a bad man*—a really *bad* young man! Papa wouldn't have your name mixed up with his for anything in the world! I know you can't be convinced, just now, because you've come through an unusual experience together, and I'm sure I'm glad if he was half decent. It wasn't to be expected, though it's what I've always claimed, that a really nice girl always has the upper hand of a man, even a bad man, and he dare not be rude to her. Then, of course, it was quite thoughtful of him to leave those roses the way he did and go away without any message. I'll give him credit for that. But it was most unfortunate that he should have been the one to save you! Papa would not at all approve of your having anything more to do with him whatever."

"That is just what he said," said Jean quietly.

"What *he* said!" exclaimed her sister. "Really! Then he does realize a little what people think of him! Well, that is a commendable attitude, of course, and if you think it necessary, you might write a formal little note, very brief, and thank him for bringing you home, but make him understand that he is not to presume . . . or, if you prefer, I might do it for you. On second thought I think Mamma would prefer that I . . ."

"It is not in the least necessary, Eleanor; I have thanked Mr. Holt already, and he understands perfectly that it would not be agreeable to you to have him come here. You said you had sewing to do, don't you want me to help you with something? I'd love to."

There was a dignity in the set of the head and the firm curve of lip that made Mrs. Harrington survey her young sister with wonder and silence as they arose and went toward the house. The way Jean had set aside the topic of young Holt was masterly. Mrs. Harrington had not said nearly all she meant to say on the subject, but somehow she did not see the way clear to open the subject again at present. She looked at Jean uneasily from time to time as they sat together in the house, or went about from room to room, flying from one topic to another as people will do who have been long separated. Three distinct times did Mrs. Harrington essay to give an extended dissertation on the evil deeds and reputation of Jasper Holt, and each time the subject was as summarily closed, and quietly set aside by Jean as if she had no interest whatever in the young man. It gave the woman almost an uncanny feeling, and actually disturbed her seriously, so that she was threatened with one of her nervous headaches. After lunch, having had to confess to her husband that she had made no headway in doing his bidding about enlightening her sister with regard to his enemy, she retired to her darkened room to sleep. Jean, glad of escape to quiet, fled to her roses.

Broodingly, as a mother would touch her little child while it sleeps, Jean hovered over those flowers. The door was locked safe from intrusion, and the children sent to a neighbor's that the house might be quiet. She drew the little table near the great window chair, and placed the bowl of roses upon it.

They filled the bowl, lying heavy-headed in great sheaves over its rim on their cool, luscious leaves, those leaves of that peculiar green touched with burnt sienna on tips and veins, that speak of a high state of cultivation, and rare stock. She laid her cheek against the cool yellow of the flowers, then her lips, then her closed eyelids, while she let her thoughts rove back to yesterday, and the time when their giver had been at her side; the words he had spoken, the way he had looked, the sound of his voice, and the firm clasp of his hand. It all rushed over her in a tumult of joy and sorrow.

This was the man she knew, so kind, so tender, so strong, so true; and that other was the one *they thought he was!* She could never feel that way about him no matter *what* people told her, for she had seen what they had not. If they had been there in her place and he had been that strong companion and friend they might have understood. She would, of course, respect their wishes, and not do anything to trouble those who loved her; but she would trust him always.

And now there stirred in her mind the remembrance of that paper, the disposition of which she must decide at once. How should she get it to him? It would not do to send for him. He could not, probably *would* not, come if she did. Even a letter which did not explain too much would be a difficult thing to manage, at least until she knew the way to the post office and could mail it herself. If it were carried by a servant or a member of the family, it might be subject to inspection. Yet the paper ought to go to him at once. Still, of course, in her keeping it was at least out of his enemies' hands, if enemies they were, these dear people of her own family. Oh, why were things at once so bitter and so sweet in this hard, bright world? She buried her face in the roses again and let their sweetness rush over her. As she did so a slight rustling sound startled her, and when she lifted up her face and then pressed it close again she heard it once more. Curious, with a wild fleeting hope floating through her brain, she sat up and began to touch the buds and blossoms softly, eagerly, searchingly with her fingers. Yes, there it was, that sound of crackling paper!

She folded back the petals of the largest bud, and there, laid deftly in like another flower-leaf, she found a tiny bit of folded paper. Eagerly she took it out and opened it, for it was very thin and folded close, and there was writing, small and fine, but boldly, distinctly clear:

"I have to go away. For how long I do not know. I shall not forget my promise. You may trust me. I hope you have a happy time."

The tears were in her eyes as she read the brief message over and over again, and laid her lips upon it. Bright drops fell upon the roses and stood like dew drops.

She searched the other blossoms carefully, but there were no more messages, and she had known there would not be. He would not think it "square" to write more of the things that were in his heart, and she loved him the more for his sense of honor toward her.

Then she remembered the water contract.

Now, what should she do with the paper? She could not give it to him while he was away. It might await his return and be lost if she trusted it to the mail. She must wait for a few days and see if he came back; and meantime she would listen and watch as far as it lay in her power, that no harm came near his rights. If worse came to worst she would confide in her father. He was wise, and he would understand. He would feel as she did about this matter if he knew all. The difficulty would be to make him know all through the medium of a mere letter. But for the present she would wait.

A sense of desolation settled down upon her when she realized that Holt was gone away; yet she was at peace about it. At least she need not always be fearing lest her relatives should be unpleasant to him, or that embarrassing circumstances might arise where she would be obliged to choose between her sense of loyalty to Holt and her sense of loyalty to her relatives in whose home she was a guest. But for a little time she put away these thoughts and let her happy heart dwell on the fact that he had sent these glorious roses with their secret message; and finally she lay down for a rest and slept, with one great yellow bud nestled against her cheek.

Chapter 13

The days which followed fulfilled all Mrs. Harrington's prophecies so far as gaiety was concerned. One round of pleasure succeeded another. The days were filled with picnics and rides and the evenings with merrymaking of all descriptions at all the houses in the region about Hawk Valley. There were many young officers and others who were eager to teach the sweet young stranger from the east to ride. Horses especially trained and gentled for her use were brought as offerings at her shrine, and flowers from near and far were sent to her. The Harrington children were in danger of becoming chronic dyspeptics on the surplus of the confections with which she was constantly supplied; and there was no opportunity for her to become lonely or morbid as the summer days sped by in a round of pleasure.

Yet through it all Jean moved, lovely and serene as a summer morning.

"She acts as if she had been in society for years," complained Eleanor to her husband. "Nothing moves her out of her quiet dignity. She doesn't gush or become enthusiastic at anybody. The sky and the flowers and the children please her more than all the adulation she receives. One would almost judge her engaged or married already. I wonder if it can be there is a sweetheart at home that we don't know about. I must write and ask Mamma. I can't make it out. I thought Captain Hawthorne would surely make an impression, he has such charming manners, and is so deferential to women; but she looked at him today with that sweet faraway expression, exactly as she might have looked at her grandfather. Of course it made him desperately determined

118

to get her attention, but she never seemed to know nor care. One would almost think it was a studied pose to get as many at her feet as possible, if one didn't know Jean better."

"Did you ever think that perhaps her thoughts are with that scoundrel Holt?" her husband asked.

"Nonsense!" said his wife sharply. "She never mentions him. She has forgotten all about him. I think she was extremely annoyed at our making so much of his bringing her home."

"Well, don't you be too sure. I wonder where the deuce he is. I'll be willing to bet he's up to some mischief."

"Don't worry," said his wife, "I'm only too glad he's taken himself away. I hope he'll keep hidden until Jean is safely home again so we won't be annoyed."

"I hope he'll come back and let us see what he's up to," growled her husband as she left the room.

And at last one day shortly before Jean was to return to her father's house, Holt came back.

With him appeared Scathlin, riding into town daily, side by side with the younger man, on one of Holt's horses; looking older, with a sheepish expression and a shifty eye that failed to meet men's gaze. It was rumored that Holt had found him with a broken leg, nursed him into strength again and brought him home. Those who knew Scathlin felt that Holt's power over him was more than that of gratitude.

It happened that Jean was riding with the Captain one morning when they came down to the post office together, and the glad smile with which she greeted Holt was followed by a frightened expression as she recognized Scathlin. Her escort was so astonished at having to lift his hat to Holt that he failed to notice her startled glance.

No one could have told by Holt's grave bow that he was meeting the one of all the earth to him. Only the light in his eyes told of his joy in seeing her once more, and reassured the girl as she glanced from Scathlin back to his own face. It

was Captain Hawthorne's annoyed drawl that recalled her
to the present out of the whirl of joy that the sight of Holt
brought.

"Where in the world did you ever meet that scoundrel
that he should presume to speak to you?"

A flush of indignation rose to her cheeks, her chin tilted
just the slightest bit haughtily, and her eyes held a dangerous light on them.

"Excuse me, Captain Hawthorne, Mr. Holt is my friend.
He did me the greatest service one can do for another. He
saved my life."

"I beg your pardon, Miss Grayson, I didn't mean to offend you. That alters the case of course. One is always grateful for one's life, and may thank even a dog. You can afford
to be generous, sometimes, but have a care! You do not
know Holt! It's the only good thing I ever heard of him, that
he saved your life. I would it had been my privilege instead
of his."

"Thank you, Captain Hawthorne," Jean spoke frigidly,
"but you misunderstand me. I am not speaking to Mr. Holt
because I am grateful or generous, but because I honor and
trust him as a friend."

"You do not know him, Miss Grayson. He is not a man
whom anyone trusts."

"It is *you* who do not know him, Captain Hawthorne. I
know him better than you, and I trust him entirely. During
our terrible experience together at the time of the wreck I
had ample opportunity to test Mr. Holt, and I found him a
gentleman and a true friend in every trying situation."

And now indeed Jean's tone was unmistakable, and the
alarmed Captain, who had congratulated himself that he
was making pretty good headway with the fair lady, made
hasty apologies.

"I beg your pardon, of course," he said humbly. "I'm glad
to hear that he behaved decently. To tell you the truth I
don't know much personally about Holt. I've only taken

what others say; and I've always thought his reckless appearance bore out their insinuations. Forgive me if I have annoyed you, and try to forget what I've said. This day is perfect and the road is particularly fine. Shall we try a gallop?"

Jean was glad of the relief from conversation, and kept her horse on a wild gait most of the way; for her mind was in a tumult. How was she to get that paper to Holt and what should she say in explanation of its being in her possession? The question had been much in her mind during Holt's absence, and she had been unable to decide just what she should do when he returned, but now it must be decided at once, for there ought to be no delay about the paper. The sinister look in the faded blue eyes of Scathlin as he looked at her made her fear to keep it in her possession any longer.

The ride at last was ended. It had not been a very great success from the Captain's point of view and he went away dejected, while Jean hurried to her room and tried to plan what to do. The sight of Scathlin worried her. If the old man knew what papers the wallet had contained he probably knew the significance of each. The conversation she had overheard seemed to include him in the plot, if plot there was, against Holt. Of course, since he had returned, he would seek out the other two men and explain why he had sent the wallet; and perhaps he had the other missing paper himself, the one that contained valuable information about the location of ore. It was even possible that he knew already that she, his unwilling messenger, had the water contract. He must have known it was in the wallet when he gave it to her and it would be entirely natural for him to think she had taken it out. Something in the gleam of his eye as he looked at her had made her tremble; and she longed to fly straight to Holt and give him the paper frankly and openly, but it was a matter that could not be handled openly, and she was not a diplomat; therefore she trembled.

Finally, after careful thought, and much writing and tear-

ing up of what she had written she framed a brief note to
Holt.

On the morning that she mailed it Scathlin happened to
be in the village.

Holt had gone away very early in the morning, on a matter of business, leaving word that he might not return until
the next day, and Scathlin felt like a prisoner let out of jail.
It was his first opportunity to go about without Holt's eyes
upon him. True, he was under oath to do and not to do certain things, with penalty of a judgment which he knew
would not be light. Yet his natural cunning found many
ways to carry on his schemes without violating the letter of
his contract with Holt. He knew that Holt had brought him
there as a witness against his enemies in the case of the stolen papers. He knew this, though Holt had said no word of it
to him. He also knew that Holt would watch him closely—
that he probably had him under surveillance even during
this brief absence; yet he longed to outwit his keeper and get
the better of him. If it only had not been for the loss of that
water contract his way would have been plain. He had already managed an interview with Harrington and learned
the facts without revealing all the facts in his own possession. He professed to Harrington that *all* the original
papers were in the wallet when he gave it to the girl, and
that it had been his only hope of saving them from Holt.
That Holt had managed to save the girl and bring her home
only proved that he was as hard to get away from as the
devil himself. This explanation Scathlin devised while he
listened to Harrington's story, secretly realizing, with bitterness, his own blunder in leaving the water contract in the
wallet. His excuse was that he had no time to take out another paper and secrete it safely before Holt saw him.

Night and day Scathlin worried over that water contract,
coming always back to the conclusion that Holt must have it
or know where it was; and he had searched every available
hiding place in Holt's house for it, but failed as yet to dis-

cover it. When they met Jean riding, the old man had noted carefully the expression on his companion's face as he touched his hat to her, and the lighting up of the girl's face. His keen little eyes searched, and found an idea.

Therefore, that first morning of his freedom from Holt, when he sat on the curbstone with one of the men from the Divide, talking over the latest cattle stealing, his eye took in with keen interest the figure of Jean coming down the street accompanied by her little niece, a bundle of letters in her hand to be mailed. He watched her furtively as she passed him, though she did not see him, and as soon as she was inside the post office door he got up hurriedly and followed her, professing that he had an errand.

He watched her slipping her letters one by one into the mail box, and kept his eye upon her as she turned and went out again.

He made a small purchase at the counter on the other side of the post office room, and went out. An hour later, when he returned that way, the postmaster leaned from his window and called him. "Hey, there, Scathlin, goin' up home? Here's a letter fer Holt."

Scathlin, wary as any fox, concealed the start he almost gave, and turned with indifference.

" 'Spose I might's well take it," he said, and receiving the letter, went on his way toward home.

The way was long and bright and hot, and Scathlin was not feeling up to a hard walk yet after his weeks in bed; but he managed it in an incredibly short space of time, and as he walked he studied that letter.

It was dainty and white, the writing unmistakably feminine, and mailed in Hawk Valley. Scathlin's imagination stirred within him, and he was almost sure he needed to know what was in that letter. He held it up to the light but nothing was revealed. He tried to pry open a corner of the flap that was not closely sealed, and squint in, but not a glimpse of writing was visible. He went home, laid it on the desk in Holt's office and sat down to watch it and think. Then just before the return for dinner of the other two men who were about the place he quietly put it in his pocket. He preferred to think about that letter awhile longer before anyone else saw it. When they came in Scathlin had the fire going and a fine steam ascending from the teakettle, an unusual attention on his part toward other members of his group, unless he was pressed to service.

But Scathlin had exhausted his capacity for work with putting on the teakettle. He sat dreamily meditating in a chair tilted back against the wall, his feet on the rounds, a straw in his mouth, and his eyes narrow and gleaming.

"Dear friend: I have something that I am sure belongs to you. Is it safe for me to send it to you through the mail? I think it must be valuable. Please let me know quickly for I am going home in a few days."

Those were the magic words the steam had revealed to Scathlin, and on which he meditated with his eyes half closed while his companions scornfully cooked the cornbread and bacon and cursed him for a lazy good-for-nothing. He continued his meditations unmoved until the men had eaten and were gone on their way. When they were out of sight he arose with alacrity and prepared a hasty meal, keeping his eye on the clock. He ate hurriedly, cleaned and loaded a pistol which he took from a hiding place behind a loose brick of the chimney, and went out the back door toward the woods.

About the same time Jean Grayson mounted the pony that had been set aside for her use while in Hawk Valley, and started out for her daily call on an old lady who had taken a great fancy to her, because of her likeness to a daughter long since dead. She was fond of the sweet old lady, and found her quiet little home a refuge from the round of society that sometimes became almost oppressive at her sister's house. She had discovered that she could avoid certain annoyingly frequent callers by being thus absent a little while, and especially during the last two weeks she had made this pleasant pilgrimage almost every day. Perhaps a part of the pleasantness of the trip was in the fact that the road lay back of Holt's land, and his house, though almost a mile from where she had to pass, was plainly to be seen at one high point on the road. It stood boldly against the sky, its wide verandas shrouded in rose vines.

Jean never ventured on the road that led past the house itself, for it was off the general highway; but she had often longed to see the spot where he lived at closer range.

As she rode along she mused about the letter she had written and whether that had been the right way and the only way to go about getting the paper into the hands of its owner.

She had once heard a great speaker say that there was never a situation where there was not a right thing to do next. She felt sure she had done the right thing so far as her light showed her; and yet she could not lay it aside and be at peace, but was in a tremor of excitement awaiting Holt's reply.

As she reached the high point in the road she looked as usual off toward the rose-vined dwelling, half hoping to see a sign of the master of the house; but the vines lay shimmering in the sun of the warm midday, and nothing seemed stirring about the place. She walked the pony slowly along until the house was out of sight, and the road entered the shady quiet where wooded land on either side hid the glare of the afternoon. Just beyond the woods a few rods away was the home of the old lady. It was early yet and Jean lingered, the pony nothing loath to follow her will.

They had gone perhaps fifty feet into the shadow of the wooded road when suddenly, out from behind a great tree with stocky, brushwood growth around it, slunk forth Scathlin, close to the pony, and laid hands upon his bridle.

"I beg pardon, Miss, but Mr. Holt sent me on a message,"

lied Scathlin, shifting his eyes hastily from the clear ones
that looked in horror upon him.

Jean's heart was beating wildly, not reassured by his
words.

"He said would you please give me the paper you had
for him. It would be safer for me to get it, as no one would
suspect."

A great doubt seized Jean's soul. Holt had not sent this
bad old man. Holt could never trust such a man at this. But
if he did trust him, *she* did not.

"Did Mr. Holt send me a letter?" Jean looked keenly into
the old cunning face.

"Mr. Holt had to go away in a hurry and so he sent me,"
said Scathlin glibly. "He didn't have no time to write letters.
He said you knowed me; that you'd seen me with him, an'
you'd know 'twas all right."

"Tell Mr. Holt, please," said Jean, making up her mind
hurriedly, "that there is nothing, and no message I can give
to anyone. I wish to speak with him. If that is not possible,
we will have to let the matter pass."

She drew the rein and signed to her horse to go on, but
Scathlin jerked the bridle sharply.

"Not much, you don't go on," he threatened, "not till I get
that paper. I was sent here to get it and I mean to have it.
You can't play any of your pretty little tricks on me. I want
that paper and I mean to have it. Ef I can't get it one way I
kin another!" His voice and eyes were ominous, and Jean
was so frightened that her throat trembled and she could
scarcely control her lips to speak.

"Of what paper are you speaking?"

"That there paper you wrote about in the letter. You
know well enough what I mean. You've got it about you
now. I know you dassent go off and leave it to home, where
that fine brother-in-law of yours could find it. Come, are
you going to fork over, or do you want me to search you for
it? I'll find it quick enough."

Chapter 14

Jean turned white with deadly sickening fear, but kept her head courageously up. She whipped up her pony and tried to get away, but the strong hand held the bridle and the little beast could only rear, almost throwing her. Moreover, a gleaming pistol shone into Jean's terrified eyes, and Scathlin in gloating voice spoke low.

"Oh, no, my pretty, you don't play any of your little tricks on me. You've stole a paper I give you to give to your brother-in-law, an' I mean to have it without any further nonsense. Hand it over!" and he grasped her roughly by the arm.

"Help! Mr. Holt! *Jasper!*" she screamed.

Something was stuffed into her mouth and the barrel of the pistol gleamed between her eyes. She could feel the cold steel against her flesh. The earth seemed reeling beneath her, and her senses were going from her. Was there no hope of help from anywhere?

"Now, my pretty, I'll just help myself to that paper." Scathlin's voice was malevolent, his eyes gleaming. Like the cold slimy length of a serpent coiling around her soul, the meaning of his words slid about her consciousness. She felt she was sinking out of the world of knowledge into a blackness where she could not protect herself.

Then quickly, sharply, a voice brought her back to consciousness.

"Drop that pistol! Let go of that lady! Now, *march!*"

It was Holt's voice, low, merciless, commanding; and a revolver was in his hand.

Scathlin fell away like water, turning deadly white and cringing. The day of his judgment had come swiftly, and there was no escape. He knew that look in Holt's eye. He had sinned away his last probation. Holt would never trust him again. There was not even time to destroy the letter which he had wanted to keep and give to Harrington as evidence against the girl.

"March!" said Holt's voice again, and the revolver came uncomfortably near to Scathlin's temple.

Scathlin marched.

"Go straight to the house and wait there till I come," commanded Holt as Scathlin backed weakly away. "If you attempt to escape I'll turn the bloodhounds loose after you."

Scathlin turned a shade paler. He had had experience with one of those bloodhounds. He had no desire to meet the whole pack. He hastened his footsteps.

Jean sat with wild eyes watching, her hand upon her heart.

"You didn't send him for the paper, did you?" she demanded eagerly. "I knew you would never have sent him."

"Send for the paper, what paper?" asked Holt in wonder. "I never sent him for anything."

"Then how did he know what was in my letter to you?"

"Letter? What letter? I never received a letter from you."

"Then he must have opened it and read it. Oh, *he will show it to my brother-in-law!*"

But Holt's voice rang out clearly before her sentence was fairly finished. "Halt! Scathlin!"

Scathlin had almost reached the turning at the edge of the woods, but he paused instantly.

"Come back here."

Scathlin came, cringing and white with fear. When he was within ten yards of the two Holt spoke again, and all the time the sinister weapon kept guard in his hand aimed straight at Scathlin.

"Give me my letter."

"W-what l-let-tt-ter?" chattered Scathlin with ill concealed attempt to use his cunning.

"The letter you have in your pocket. Take it out instantly

and drop it on the ground or I shall fire," said Holt sternly.

"Well, put down that gun," whimpered Scathlin, fumbling nervously in his inside pocket, "you make me n-n-nervous!"

"Be quick! Drop that letter!" said Holt, still holding the revolver.

Scathlin took out the letter and dropped it on the ground, but his bad little eyes gleamed green and yellow hate at the girl in one look of wrath as he turned and stumbled back again.

Holt, still holding the revolver and watching the retreating man, advanced and picked up the letter. When Scathlin was out of sight he read it, then turned with softened eyes to the girl who had meantime secured the paper from its hiding place pinned within her blouse. She held it out to him, her hand still trembling with the fright she had been through.

Holt took the paper, but gathered the little hand into his tenderly and, stooping, kissed it.

"To think you have been through all this for me." There was awe in his voice. "To think you trusted me instead of your own people!"

For an instant they looked into each other's eyes; then Holt's horse, trained to stand and await his master's will, whinnied softly.

"We must not stand here," said Holt, looking up sharply, "someone might come. I will take you on to Mrs. Foster's, and then go back and see that Scathlin is where he can do no further harm. How long will you wish to be there? Can you stay an hour and then ride back? I will be waiting just in the shadow of the woods and see you to the edge of town where you will be safe. Please don't ride out of town alone again."

"But I shall not be afraid to go back," protested Jean. "You need not take all that trouble. Now that you have the paper I shall not be afraid."

"Trouble!" said Holt, looking at her with eyes that adored. "You know it is no trouble. But what is this paper that has made so much disturbance?" He had mounted his horse and was riding by her side now. He unfolded the paper, but it needed only a glance to show him what it was.

"How did you happen to have it?" he asked, looking at her startled. "Have you the others?"

"No," she said, a cloud of trouble coming into her eyes. "I had them, I suppose, but I did not know they were yours. I had the wallet, with them in. That man gave them to me on the train before the wreck. You picked the wallet up once when it fell, don't you remember? Didn't you know they were yours?"

"Yes," said Holt, "I knew. At least I supposed I knew."

"Why didn't you tell me?"

"I didn't want to mix you up in the trouble," he said, looking at her tenderly, "and besides, I knew they were safe in your possession for the present."

"But they weren't. I didn't know they were yours, and I gave them to my brother-in-law."

"I knew you would, of course. But I was pretty sure I could stop any harm he would do before he could do it. The only thing I was troubled about was this paper. I didn't think Scathlin was fool enough to leave all the papers in the wallet. I was pretty sure he had kept this and one other himself and only sent the rest back to throw me off the track and make me think he had sent all of them. He knew I saw him give you the wallet and he meant I should see. He thought I would stop watching him and give my attention to you, but I knew Scathlin better than that. I kept my eye on him. But how did you happen to have this one paper?"

"I'm not sure. When I came back to my room, after giving James the wallet, I found this on my floor. It may have fallen when I dumped the things out of my bag. The wallet fell apart and all the papers went out on the table, but I thought I picked up every one. Then when I came back to my room I found this on the floor just as I was about to turn out the light. Later I overheard a conversation in which this paper and another were described as missing. The other was something to do with a mine."

"Yes, I have it," said Holt.

"You *have* it? *Oh,* I am so glad! Then they can't trouble your claim, can they? I suppose that was what they meant, I'm not very much of a business person. But how did you get it? They said it was in the wallet."

"It was," said Holt, "till Scathlin took it out. I think he intended taking this, also, and leaving with you only the other papers which were utterly valueless without these two; but he had to work quickly while I was at the other end of the car, and he blundered. I got it out of Scathlin's shoe, just after the accident occurred, and before I left the car we were in. We had a struggle in the dark, but I secured my paper before he flung me off and crawled out of the window. After that, I lost sight of him. I was hunting for him in the water when I found you. I didn't know who you were till I drew you up on the bank. But I never dreamed you had this paper. I thought, of course, it was still with Scathlin. That is why I was away so long, hunting him. I didn't know once but I'd lost him completely, but I finally got on his track. I was sure he knew where this paper was and I didn't dare to lose him. I brought him home to watch him; and I've kept him in sight all day today. He thought I was away from home for two days, but I've been in hiding. I had him watched when he went to town and I knew he came home. If he had had this paper he would have gone straight to your brother-in-law. A field glass and a whistle will do a good deal to keep track of a man. When he stole out of the house towards the woods I knew something was happening and signaled my men. They are waiting now. They'll look after Scathlin till I get back."

He raised a tiny whistle to his lips and blew a long, silvery blast, followed by two more, and in a moment there came back two answers from slightly different directions.

They were come now to the open road, and Holt drew his

horse to one side. Mrs. Foster's home was but a stone's throw away and she was sitting on the porch in her reclining chair.

"I will be here when you are ready to go home," said Holt, looking at her tenderly; then, touching his hat, he wheeled his horse and was out of sight in a twinkling.

The next hour was always a blur in the memory of Jean. Somehow she drew her senses together and dismounted at her friend's door, going through the formalities of meeting, and adjusting herself to the occasion; but not for an instant did her subconscious cease to rehearse the events just passed. Her whole body quivered again with the fear that swept over her at sight of Scathlin; she shrank once more from his touch as the full realization of her escape was made known to her; and the look and voice of Holt thrilled her as nothing had ever done in her life. How could they say he was not good when he was like that? She had seen the soul of him looking out of his wonderful eyes and she knew. But how had it come about that others had not seen, also? Oh, if they knew once; if they could just get a real glimpse of the true man, they would never again feel as they did about him.

She recognized fully the separation there was between them and it brought a constriction of tears in her throat; but in her heart was a glad glow that he cared for her, and for the time it seemed enough to fill her with deep joy. She was going to see him again in a few minutes, and she could thank him for saving her life again, this time perhaps from something worse than death. She had had no words wherewith to tell him of the infinite relief his appearing had brought; everything had happened so quickly; but it seemed as if a lifetime would be too brief to voice her gratitude for her deliverance. She shivered as she remembered the look on Scathlin's face when he took hold of her.

Mrs. Foster said: "Why, you're not cold, are you, dearie, this warm day? I believe they are letting you do too much, with all their parties and things. You look white. You'd better come down and stay with me a week and get rested up."

But Jean's laugh rang silverly.

"Oh, no, I'm not cold, Mrs. Foster, I'm just glad over something. It's very nice of you to ask me to visit you, and I would be delighted, but you know I'm going home next week, and I'm afraid Eleanor wouldn't want to spare me when the time is so short."

"Going home next week!" exclaimed the old lady, in dismay. "Why, I thought you were going to stay till Christmas."

"So I was, but Father has to go to New York to a convention. He's been made a delegate, and it's a splendid thing for him. He hasn't had an outing in a long time. He needs it; and we couldn't leave Mother alone you know. Mother is an invalid. So of course I'm going home a little sooner. But I've had a beautiful time here, and maybe I can come again sometime."

All the time that Jean was talking her real self was thinking how wonderful it had been that it was Holt who saved her again and not just some passing stranger.

The hour was over at last and Jean joyously mounted her pony and bade her friend good-bye; but when she rode into the shadow of the woods and saw Holt on his shining black horse waiting quietly beside the road for her, a great shyness overcame her, and she knew she would never be able to put into words the great thoughts of her heart, and that perhaps it was as well; for he would understand and words were not necessary for them. There could not be much said without saying too much.

After all they said very little. The way was short till they came to the edge of town though they walked their horses as slowly as possible; but there were looks and glances of the soul, trustful, grateful, worshipful; and each felt the blessedness of these few minutes alone together.

Holt told her briefly of Scathlin. He was safe. She need fear him no more. He would not be abroad to trouble her during the rest of her stay. His eyes more than his words informed her how he regretted the brevity of that stay. His eyes told her also that Scathlin's judgment would be tempered with mercy and righteousness.

There was one question she wished to ask him. She hesitated long but finally risked it.

"You will enter the tournament?" she asked, lifting her eyes full of pleading that his answer should be yes. "You know about it, of course? You know they are giving me a tournament before I go home?"

He bowed gravely.

"Yes, I know. You will like it. It is one of the most interesting affairs they have in town. I am glad you will see it."

She saw he was evading her question.

"You will enter?" she asked again anxiously.

He searched her face keenly.

"You want me to?"

"I do, very much," she said, and the rich color in her cheeks told him how much she wanted it.

"Your friends will not like it," he said.

"But the tournament is given for me, and I shall like it," she said with spirit. "I am sure you can ride."

"I can ride a little," he said indifferently.

"Then you will enter?"

"If you really wish it."

"I certainly wish it," she said gladly.

Then suddenly out from the woods rode two men; fine, tall, sturdy fellows they were, perhaps ten or more years older than Holt, but with strong faces, keen eyes, and muscles that looked like iron.

They saluted Holt as if he were their military officer, and one rode close to him and said a few words in a low tone. Holt nodded gravely, his fine, boyish face taking on maturer lines as he gave attention to the message, and uttered his brief, ready directions, utterly unintelligible to the girl who

looked on in bewilderment at this new phase of the young
man's character.

The second rider had halted at a respectful distance,
without a glance in her direction, and waited as a trained
servitor should do. Devotion to Holt and absolute obedience
were in the attitude of both.

The interview occupied scarcely a minute; then the two
men wheeled, saluted, and rode away once more into the
woods.

"A little trouble at the mine," Holt explained, in answer
to her questioning glance. "It'll be all right now, since I have
this paper again. We haven't dared to exercise our water
privileges as we should and have been moving under diffi-
culties, but now that I have the grant there will be no further
trouble. I'll take care it's put where no one can steal it
again."

"Oh, I'm so glad," breathed Jean, "but who are they?"
pointing after the two riders who were just disappearing behind the trees.

"My men," said Holt. "I have fifty-four of them, fine fellows everyone."

"Your men?" questioned Jean in surprise.

"They work for me in the mine and around the place. I've
picked them up here and there. That big fellow that
waited—I took him down from a tree where they'd hung
him up for stealing a horse. He's the one I told you of—I
thought he was dead, but there he is! He wouldn't take a pin
now that belonged to anyone else. He's the straightest fellow
on the place. The other one was almost gone with fever
when I met up with him. We've nursed each other twice
apiece since then. There are others I'd like you to know if
things weren't as they are. You'd see the good in them, I'm
sure. You seem to understand."

Jean's eyes were alight as she watched him.

"They know you!" she exclaimed. "They've seen the real
you, and they trust you! I saw it in their eyes."

"Maybe," he said, returning her look. "They'd fight for me anytime I asked it; and they'd die for me if it came to that."

"Greater love hath no man than this, that a man lay down his life for his friends." The words seemed to come of themselves from the girl's lips as she watched the man in wonder and admiration.

"You took a mighty slim chance on your's for me about an hour ago." Holt's eyes spoke volumes. "Why didn't you give him the paper? It was by far the safest thing for you to do. Didn't you know that?"

"Yes," said the girl, her soft lips setting in a firm line and her chin taking the tilt that gave her sweet face its strength and fineness. "But the paper was yours, and I was sure it was valuable. I didn't trust him."

"And you trust me yet, in spite of all the things I know you must have heard about me?"

"I'll trust you *forever!*"

Her eyes were clear and steady, and her voice was sweet with a ring of triumph in it as she made the declaration.

For a moment they looked at one another with a great blinding light of deep gladness shining from their eyes; then the man bowed his head gravely and, reaching over, took her hand in a strong, quick clasp.

"You shall never have cause to lose that trust," he murmured solemnly, and turning, rode back into the woods and left her to go on alone through the town.

Chapter 15

When Jean reached the Harrington home she found a group of girls on the piazza waiting for her, who chattered and laughed and took absolute possession of her. They were planning an all-day trip on horseback with lunches and all sorts of interesting things by the way, and Jean must help them. They gave her no chance to speak, but told her all in chorus, until she could scarcely make out what it was about. She smiled and agreed, but half the time she did not know what they were saying, for something still and beautiful within her soul was claiming her attention, something that seemed too high and holy to be affected by any of these foolish little things wherewith the others wanted to while away the time—the brief, dear time left her to be in *his* neighborhood. Yet she smiled and agreed, and they all thought her charming, and went on making their plans.

They made out their list of men who were to be invited. She heard the names read, and took no account of whom they had selected for her escort. What did it matter? *His* name was not among them! She heard their talk about their horses.

"Robin Hood has gone lame," declared one girl pettishly, "isn't that a shame? Father says it's my fault, but I know better. He's going to get me a new horse pretty soon when he can find one to suit him. I know just the one I want, coal black and shines like satin. He can go like the wind and take a river as if he had wings. I'm dead in love with him. I'm just dying to ride him, but his owner won't sell him. Isn't that mean? He belongs to Jasper Holt. Father has offered him a fabulous price, but he won't sell him at any price, he says. I think he's perfectly horrid. Of course he only does it just to be disagreeable because he thinks I want him. That man makes me tired!"

There was a soft color on Jean's cheeks and she looked up as if a challenge to defend her friend had been flung to her.

"Perhaps he's fond of the horse," she said gently, as she glanced around on all those scornful young faces.

"He, fond of anything! Oh, my dear! You don't know him!" declared one of the girls.

"He never was fond of anything in his life," laughed another. "Why, he's the cruelest thing! You don't know, Jean."

"Men grow very fond of horses," said Jean, holding her head high and the roses in her cheeks deepening, "and their horses grow fond of them. A horse loves one who is kind to him."

She was remembering the proud arch of Jasper Holt's black as he rode beside her in the woods but a short half hour before.

Her words were met by a shout of merriment, and a boisterous young voice with a sneer in it pierced above the laughter.

"Kind to them! Jasper Holt was never kind to anything in his life! My dear, you simply don't know him!"

"But I *do* know him!" said Jean now, rising from her rocker and standing slim and straight against the vine-covered pillar of the porch. "I know him better than you all, and I know he *is* kind. He was kind and splendid to me! No man could have done more! I am sorry you feel that way about him. It isn't right! He is my friend!"

She had spoken! She had always meant to, ever since she came; but there had been little opportunity without being deliberately disagreeable and dragging the subject in. Perhaps Eleanor had warned her callers not to mention Jasper Holt, for they usually seemed to avoid speaking of him; but she had always felt the time would come when she could speak and let them all know what she thought about him, and now it had come and she had spoken. Her heart beat wildly, her cheeks were rosy red, and her eyes shining starrily, but she stood unabashed and faced them all.

A sudden silence fell upon the little group and they exchanged furtive glances of understanding as if a mutual agreement sealed their lips to things that they might say if she were not with them.

"Oh, well, of course you're grateful," said one girl in a conciliatory tone. "One couldn't help being grateful under such circumstances; but he would have been a brute not to have pulled you out of the water and showed you the way to Hawk Valley."

"Perhaps he wants his black to ride in the tournament," said another girl mischievously, hoping to lift the cloud that had fallen over them all. "He has audacity enough for anything, though he has never seemed to care for anything going on in the town. Of course he has never been encouraged to have."

"He wouldn't dare!" said another with flashing eyes.

"Why wouldn't he dare?" asked Jean, turning steady eyes to the haughty young speaker.

"Because it wouldn't be tolerated," declared the girl still haughtily.

"I have seen him dare greater things than that," said Jean with a faraway look in her eyes and something like a smile on her lips.

The girls looked at her a minute in silence and wonder, exchanged quick glances that said, "She does not know," and changed the subject. They liked Jean too well, and she was too popular among the men for them to risk angering her, so they chattered on about what they would have in the lunch boxes, and who should bring what; but Jean, with that faraway look in her eyes and that half smile on her lips, as if she knew things that were hidden from others, said no more.

They chattered and giggled and chorused to the end of their subject and their time at last, and took themselves away; but it was the dinner hour and Harrington was coming up the walk with two men who were to be their guests for dinner. There was just time for Jean to change her riding habit for a dinner dress and hurry down again, no chance for the rest and the quiet thoughts that cried out to have their way.

The evening was filled with callers, as every evening had been since she came that was not actually taken up by some entertainment or invitation. It seemed a wearisome time to Jean, who longed for her quiet room and her own thoughts. She watched the men who were talking to her, trying to please her; saw that they were good to look upon, cultured, and refined; saw that any one of them would be a good friend to her if she would let him; and yet, when she considered it, there was not one who came up to the standard of the man who had saved her life. She tried to look at the matter from their standpoint and understand why it was that she could not like any of them as she liked him; why they all seemed rather tedious and tiresome; and the great thought came down upon her that it was because she had first known him, and he was so much larger and finer a man in every way than they.

She had no more thought than at the beginning that she would ever see more of Holt. The future showed no bright hope that they might come together. He had said it would not do, and she trusted him. Whatever he willed concerning their friendship she bowed to, for she trusted him utterly; but there was something vivid and both strong and gentle in him that made all others vapid beside him.

She roused herself to be pleasant and entertaining, but her heart was not in it. Her sister, noticing as the evening went on that she looked white and tired, finally managed to send their guests away. And indeed, there had been moments when all the gaiety and laughter seemed far away to her, and she had only seen the evil face of Scathlin and heard his voice demanding the paper and threatening to find it for himself. Once she had shuddered and shivered visibly as if she were chilly, and the Captain hastened to pick up a gauze scarf and throw it around her shoulders, while Freeman Thorne pulled down the window.

But when they were all gone Eleanor was not at peace about her sister and in pretty negligee she came in presently to perch upon the bed and question her.

"Is anything troubling you, Jean?" she asked anxiously. "You seemed so white and tired tonight?"

"Nothing at all, dearest," said Jean brightly. "What a big responsibility I am to you, you precious big sister! You mustn't worry about me, I have had a lovely visit. But I get a little tired of talking to so many people sometimes, and having to say the same things over to all those men."

"You strange child!" said her sister, looking at her curiously. "Almost any girl would be proud to have so many admirers and you take them as a matter of course and don't seem to care a bit for any of them."

She studied the fair face of the girl keenly for any trace of self-consciousness, but Jean's smile was as placid as ever.

"They are all nice, Eleanor," said the girl wearily, "but they do grow a little tiresome; all day long some of them, and every day. I wouldn't mind if you and I had a day or two now and then just all to ourselves."

"Well, you certainly are hopeless!" said her sister. "Tell me, child, is there someone at home to whom you have given your heart?"

"Oh, no!" said Jean quickly, laughing at the thought. "Who would there be? You know all the boys, and there isn't one I could care for."

"Well, I didn't know but that new bank cashier. . . ."

"Tom Lloyd? Why he's engaged to Bella Harkness. Did no one tell you? Besides, he's years older than I am."

"Well, there's that oldest Shafton boy. Mother wrote he had come home from college and started in business. They are a good family, Jean."

"Jimmy Shafton? Oh, Eleanor! You ought to see him! He's the biggest snob! But there! I suppose he's nice enough, but I don't like him, that's all. He has a weak chin, and somehow I don't trust him. Now, Eleanor, you funny little matchmaker, just give me up as a hopeless case. You can't marry me off yet awhile and you'll have to make up your mind to it. I'm going home where I belong to take care of my mother and teach my Sunday school class; but I've had a glorious time while I was here and I shall enjoy thinking it over a lot when I get home."

Eleanor was baffled, but persistent.

"Don't you like the Captain?" she asked.

"Yes, a lot. He's going to take me for a ride through the canyon tomorrow. Will you go along? He promised to ask you."

"Well, probably he didn't want me," said Eleanor significantly.

"Well, *I* do," said Jean decidedly. "I told him I wouldn't go without you."

"Why, yes, I suppose I could take Betty on her pony."

"Do," said Jean, "I love to ride with Betty, and then you can talk to the Captain when I get tired."

"You funny little girl! Well, don't you like Freeman Thorne?"

"Of course," said Jean. "He's going to bring me some Indian arrowheads to give to my boys at home."

Eleanor sat back and surveyed her inscrutable little sister hopelessly. There was one more question she wanted to ask, but somehow she didn't dare, because she hated to see that look of hurt dignity come into Jean's eyes whenever she spoke of Jasper Holt; but there lingered in her heart just a little uneasiness about the handsome outlaw whose part the girl had so loyally taken on her arrival, and about whom her lips had remained so significantly sealed ever since. Yet, despite her uneasiness, she went to her room with the question unasked, and Jean locked her door and turned out her light with a sigh of relief that at last she was alone.

Down on her knees beside the open window she knelt, her arms on the window seat, her face raised to the eternal stars. There was a kind of triumph in her face, for though she knew the great sadness was coming rapidly on its way, yet over all the excitement of the day, the terror of peril and escape, there was a great exultation. For just this one night at least she must exult in the thought of Jasper Holt and his second saving of her life; she must rejoice in his love and the fact that she could trust him. Memory brought back now in a flood of joy every glance of his true eyes, every word and gesture, every movement and attitude of the perfect body. He seemed so much stronger and finer and nobler in every way than all those others. What a pity that he must rest under their disapproval. How dreadful that they could not know him as he really was—that she must presently go on her lonely way home, and see no more of him, know no more of him—perhaps never on this earth again. He had it in him to be true to this terrible separation because he thought it ought to be, and she was proud of him for it, but her heart already ached in anticipation of the sorrow that was in store for her.

With a sob she put her head down on the window sill and prayed softly.

"Dear God, take care of him, and help people to know him. Help him to be true always and let others find it out and be ashamed of the way they have treated him. Bless him and keep him, my dear friend!"

Then with one lingering look away to where the stars shone quietly above his dwelling as above hers, she went to sleep.

Chapter 16

The tournament was set for the day before Jean started home.

It was to be a great event, the biggest thing the town of Hawk Valley could devise in the way of entertainment for its most honored guests. It was an all-day affair, with contests and games of every kind, races and matches and a big procession with everyone wearing the brightest and most fantastic garment the resources of the town afforded.

The climax of the program was to be late in the afternoon when the great feats of riding were performed and the prizes and wreaths given out to the victors.

The highest honor had been allotted to Jean, for she had been selected to give out the prizes and crown the victor of the final riding contest.

It has been the custom heretofore in other similar contests that a lady so honored should ride once around the running track in company with the victor and share with him the triumph of the occasion. Great was the eagerness of all the young men to win this privilege on this occasion, for Jean's delicate beauty and sweet, gentle ways had made her most popular, and everyone was striving for the privilege of riding with her and being crowned by her fair hand. All in a friendly way there had been much merriment about it, much betting and chaffing, much practicing of horsemanship, much boasting, and many a gallant gentleman had besought her to wear his flowers on the gala day that he might stand the better chance of winning.

But Jean had smiled upon them all and would promise none. She took it all as a beautiful piece of pleasantry in her honor, though sometimes she was secretly distressed at the earnestness with which many of her admirers pressed their suit. They were splendid fellows, all of them, and it was hard to be refusing and disappointing them all the time. Hard, too, it was, to disappoint her sister Eleanor continually, who was an enthusiastic matchmaker and felt real chagrin that her beloved sister should go back home from all that adulation still apparently heart-free, when she had been given so many perfectly good chances to fall in love. Eleanor would have liked nothing better than to have Jean marry and settle near herself. Then the father and mother would eventually come, of course, and the family would be reunited. It was most aggravating to her that Jean remained so unimpressionable.

The day before the tournament great boxes of flowers began to arrive for Jean, embarrassing her with their riches, profusion and costliness. Orchids and lilies, gardenias and roses of rare varieties, carnations, jasmine, even delicate wild flowers and wonderful poppies. Each admirer had spent much thought and care upon his offering, hoping to have it chosen for wearing upon the great occasion; and each had tried to have his flowers unusual and noticeable enough to draw her choice away from all others. With each great box came card or note or sometimes letter bearing the name and earnest plea of the giver, three even offering themselves with their flowers.

Jean stood among her blossoms, her cheeks vying with the roses, her eyes as starry as the lilies, distressed and touched, but not quite pleased. It was terrible to her that she seemed to have wrought such havoc in the hearts of men.

Eleanor and the children hovered excitedly around, far more pleased than Jean over the honors that were heaped upon her. Eleanor talked in a high, sweet soprano about the merits of the different flowers, and the reasons why each should be worn in preference to the others.

"Here are the Captain's orchids—so expensive, poor fellow—and he is so handsome!" Eleanor always ended with

the Captain where she had begun. It was plain that Eleanor
favored the Captain most mightily.

Jean stood and touched the flowers tenderly, compassion-
ately, as though in some way they were human things that
had been cheated into coming without a cause; as she might
have looked at and touched something very beautiful that
did not belong to her. It seemed a big responsibility to have
all these lovely blossoms with all they represented, and as
she filled each vase and jar and bowl to overflowing till almost every available receptacle in the house was filled, her
eyes grew more and more troubled and thoughtful. Somehow it seemed wrong for her to have all these perishing
beauties, knowing that the lasting treasure they were here to
plead for their donors was not hers to give.

"Which flowers are you going to wear, Jean?" asked
Eleanor vexedly that night, as they went upstairs together
after tucking the blossoms all away under damp papers.
"You know you'll have to decide in the morning, and there
really aren't anymore to come in, unless Mr. Frazer sends
some. Everybody, literally every man in the region that
could have a shadow of right to do so, has sent you some. It
shows how popular you are! I don't believe any girl that ever
came here before was so well treated, and so universally admired. It's wonderful, Jean. You little, quiet, sweet child,
but you've got them all under your small thumb! I never
would have suspected it of you."

Jean smiled wearily. She was tired and her sister's idea of
triumph was not hers. It savored too much of counting the
scalps of those she had slain. She did not want to have men
at her feet to be turned away. She looked at life more
seriously than just a game where she was to win all no matter who lost.

She turned away with a gentle goodnight, and Eleanor's
eyes followed her uneasily.

"You know, you might wear one of each and satisfy them
all," she suggested.

Jean smiled and shuddered inwardly. The scalps again! A display of them!

"Never!" she murmured.

"Well, what are you going to do?" Her sister was all out of patience with her dallying.

"I'll sleep on it," she said brightly. "Aren't you tired, dear?"

And Eleanor had to let it go at that.

Young Frazer sent his flowers in the morning: wonderful violets, blue as the sky over Hawk Valley; dewy and sweet, and raised with careful tending; and there were more roses from several men at a distance who had not been reckoned upon. But Eleanor was not told of the roses that the servant found upon the doorstep when he went to sweep the piazza early in the morning; the roses with the dew upon them and the golden ruby glow of sunset in their hearts. They were not wrapped, or in a box, or accompanied by a card; nor was there even any name upon them. They simply lay upon the doorstep and made their mute appeal of fragrance; and the manservant, who, like all the other men in Hawk Valley, servant though he was, had surrendered to the gentle, beautiful girl, understood and carried them straight up to her door without telling anyone. He knew from whom they came, and he knew, by the starry look in her eyes when the others like them had come, that she would know.

She gathered them into her willing arms and thanked him. Her problem was solved, and she could go down to breakfast with a light heart.

"Have you decided which flowers to wear, Jean?" her sister asked sharply the minute she came into the room.

"Yes," said the girl with a smile, "but it's a secret. I'm not going to tell. You will see when I wear them."

Eleanor looked anxiously at the bright face with the firm lips, and the decided set of the pretty head, and sighed. She knew she would have to wait.

Jean was to go on her pony to the scene of the day's festiv-

ities, that she might be ready for the triumphal ride at the
end; and the Captain had begged the privilege of accom-
panying her, being confident that he should both see his
costly orchids adorning her, and win the right to ride home
by her side, triumphant. It seemed to him that in that case it
would be but a short way to the other heights he hoped to
attain.

He arrived at the house on the minute appointed, but
Jean, usually punctual, kept him waiting. The Harringtons
were all packed comfortably in their motorcar. They kept
calling impatiently.

"We'll be late, Jean, and James has to see about the sig-
nals and put up some more ribbons. You know he's marshal
of the day."

"Go on," called Jean sweetly from her window, "I'm just
fastening on my flowers. I'll be there in a minute. Don't
wait, we'll catch you."

They heard her footsteps flying down the stairs and Harrington started the car.

"Wait, James, I must see what flowers she chose."

"Nonsense!" said her husband, sending the car shooting
forward at a pace. "You can wait till she gets there. What
difference does it make anyway?"

"Why, if she doesn't take the right ones I can send her
back," said Eleanor, twisting her neck to see her sister, who
was just mounting her pony.

"The right ones? You don't know which ones you want
her to wear yourself; you've said so a dozen times this
morning," laughed her husband, jeeringly.

"Well, I know, but there are some quite impossible ones,
you know, and Jean is so unconventional. It would be just
like her to wear John Beard's poppies because she felt sorry
for him on account of his lameness. She always was that
way. Mamma let her choose a canary when she was little,
and she chose a poor, little faded thing that wouldn't sing a

note, because she said it wasn't pretty like the others and would enjoy a nice cage."

"Well, I guess you'll have to let her choose her own husband, anyway. She's got to live with him, and she's got a big will of her own."

"I know," said Eleanor, sighing. "I shall be relieved when she gets safely married. Mamma is so shut in that she doesn't realize how unworldly Jean is. But, James, I do wish you'd slow up a little. I must see those flowers. Betty, dear, can you tell what they are Aunt Jean is wearing?"

The little girl craned her neck.

"I think they're just roses, Mamma," said Betty indifferently.

"Roses? Are you sure, child? Aren't they orchids? The poor Captain! But there were multitudes of roses. I wonder whose they are."

They had turned into the main street, now. Banners were flying and a band playing martial music. The question of the flowers must perforce become a side issue, for there were numberless little things to be decided, and Mrs. Harrington was consulted many times before she finally mounted the grandstand and took her seat among the prominent people of the place, looking around with satisfaction to see Jean ascending the steps followed by the handsome Captain, whose dejected face still showed his disappointment about the orchids. For the moment she was too much taken up with the Captain to look closely at the wonderful roses that Jean wore; then suddenly she turned her attention to them. Where had she seen roses like those? Who could have sent them?

Then memory leaped on duty. Roses yellow as gold and with a heart of ruby! Holt's Golden Sunset! She could hear her husband's sharp voice repeating the hateful name. Could it be possible that he had had the audacity to send Jean roses on this day, when all eyes would be turned to the girl? And Jean, knowing how they felt about him, had dared to wear them!

Her cheeks grew red and her eyes flashed. She looked daggers at the girl, and then, realizing that the Captain could see her, tried to control her face; and even now Jean was moving away to the seat on the right, the seat of honor for the lady who was to present the prizes.

"Jean, wait! I must speak to you," she called. Jean, two chairs away, leaned over, smiling. Perhaps she knew what was coming, but her lips had that firm little twist as she said: "What is it?" that indicated courage to stick to a decision.

Eleanor Harrington leaned over the two chairs, speaking low and vehemently:

"Jean, take those flowers off and give them to me at once! I'll send the man back for the orchids. People will just think you have forgotten your flowers. Quick, give them to me."

Jean drew back with pretty dignity, and laid her hand protectingly over the flowers at her waist:

"I'm sorry, Eleanor," she said gently and decidedly. "I can't do what you ask. These are the flowers I intend to wear. Captain Wetherill understands me perfectly. I told him beforehand not to send me flowers."

And she turned away.

"But, Jean," cried her sister frantically, "you simply *must not* wear those roses! Send the man back for *any* others, but don't wear *those*. You don't understand! Everybody will know those are Jasper Holt's roses. People will think it very strange. Why, he isn't even here. It isn't respectable for you to have anything to do with him."

Jean looked her sister straight in the eyes.

"I understand perfectly, Eleanor," she said softly, for a group of people were coming in and taking possession of the seats around them. "I cannot and will not wear any of those other flowers."

"Then take them off entirely and don't wear any," said Eleanor, the vexed tears coming into her eyes.

"I'm sorry, Eleanor, but I must wear them," said Jean, and went quickly, almost sadly to her seat. She hated to hurt her sister, and to seem to do violence to her wishes, but the wearing of these flowers had become a thing of moment to her, a sacred duty and privilege. She knew that to Holt, if he should see her, it would be a symbol of her trust in him. If he did not come to the tournament at least she would have the satisfaction of knowing in her own heart that she had been loyal to him, in the only way vouchsafed her, that of wearing his flowers before them all.

Eleanor settled back, defeated, in her chair, two red spots glowing on her cheeks, and angry flashes in her eyes. She was mortified beyond expression. That her young sister, who had the adulation of the whole county poured at her feet, should choose, before the assembled multitude, to wear the favor of a man whom nobody recognized or favored filled her socially-aspiring soul with rage. What would James say when he found her sister had been wearing his enemy's flowers? Well, it was all James' fault anyway, for if he had kept the car waiting a minute she would have discovered Jean's folly in time to stop it. If she had seen those yellow roses glowing on her sister's gown before she mounted her pony they would never have come to the tournament, no, not if she had to detain Jean forcibly at home for the day and tell people she was taken suddenly ill! This came of bringing the girl up in a purely domestic and religious atmosphere and not teaching her a little worldly wisdom. Well, she would tell James it was his fault; that would be some satisfaction. Yes, and she would tell Jean just what she thought of her headstrong folly, too, when she got her home.

The waves of angry color had not yet ceased to flow over Eleanor's handsome face when the Thornes bustled in and took the next seats. Mrs. Thorne was a large, imposing person and had much to say of her son's admiration for Jean. She purred eagerly about the girl's beauty.

"So simple and sweet in that white dress with those beau-

tiful yellow roses! Freeman wouldn't tell me what flowers he
sent her. I wonder if they can be his. I never saw any like
them around here, did you? The boy is completely gone
about her. I suspect he spent a fabulous sum on flowers. He
sent to Kansas City for them."

It was then that Eleanor began to take heart of hope. If
Mrs. Thorne didn't know whose roses Jean wore perhaps the
other women wouldn't. Women didn't visit Jasper Holt's
home, and men didn't notice those things much.

She settled back relieved, and allowed herself to think
how well Jean was looking and how devoted the Captain
seemed in spite of his floral setback. Perhaps, after all, he
would only be the more keen that Jean was not in a hurry to
land him. Was she, after all, a little deeper than they thought
and did she plan her campaign with a view of making her
admirers all the more eager? Eleanor Harrington never had
been able to comprehend a nature higher than her own.

Chapter 17

Into the midst of Eleanor's troubled thoughts came the herald, a boy from a neighboring ranch, fantastically attired, who rode on a white pony with fluttering blue ribbons for reins, and blew three sharp blasts on a silver bugle, the signal for the opening of the sports. Eleanor Harrington whispered a few words to Betty, and helped her to slip quietly out of the seat into the aisle, then settled back relieved. She had sent a message to Jean not for anything in the world to tell anyone whose flowers she wore, and Jean looked up and smiled brightly across the heads of the people between them, nodding her consent. Betty came back to her seat, pleased to have the center of all eyes for a moment, and her mother patted her hand and reflected that, after all, it was wise in Jean not to wear any of her special admirers' flowers, for then they could none of them be angry with her; and if it should come out that she wore Holt's roses a little judicious hint of "gratitude" and "a sense of duty toward one who had saved her life" would only add charm to the lovely character of the girl. As Holt was not present what harm could come of it?

The day's sports went forward briskly. Each feature of the program had been put into separate and capable hands, and each vied with the other to make his or her stunt the best of all. There were children's games, marches and dances. There were folk dances, speeches, contests, and races of all sorts, each highly entertaining in its way; and there was the great picnic dinner when the entire company adjourned to the edge of the woods where tables had been prepared and where the good things of the town had been set forth to tempt the appetite. Everybody was hungry and everybody laughed and talked gaily.

Eleanor had had a vague hope that she might induce Jean to send home at noon for some other flowers on the plea that the ones she wore were faded, but Jean was surrounded by a company of happy young people and there really was no opportunity to speak to her. Harrington, too, who might have taken the matter in hand and convinced Jean of the error of her ways, had been summoned to the grounds to perfect some arrangement for the afternoon, so there was nothing to be done.

When the bugle blew for the afternoon program to begin Harrington was beside his wife, his work done, ready to enjoy the best part of things without anymore responsibility. But Eleanor, knowing well his moods, thought it unwise to tell him about the flowers for the present. It was too late now to change, and James would simply be furious; it was best to save that stroke about its being his fault until another time when she needed to convince him of something else.

The children had finished their entertainment in the morning, and the remainder of the program was to be done by the men.

When the first set of riders came out in line there was one among their number whom the crowd did not at first recognize; a man with bright, curly hair and fine bearing, dressed in white flannels and riding a jet black, long-limbed horse. Everywhere among the seats could be heard the murmur: "Who is he?" but no one answered.

Harrington raised his field glass and looked; then dropped his hand with an exclamation of dismay. Eleanor, watching her husband's face, reached for the glass, looked a moment, then she too dropped the glass in her lap and gave her attention to controlling her countenance. No one must suspect what a bitter drop in the day's cup of pleasure this was to them.

Harrington sat, grimly reflecting that he might have prevented this possibility if he had framed the entrance qualifications aright; but Holt had been away indefinitely when the tournament was planned and he had not thought of him. Now it was too late to do a thing; and there were reasons that made it unwise for him to show displeasure or unfriendliness to Holt, lest suspicion of a worse character fall upon himself.

For the remainder of the afternoon life to Eleanor Harrington became a matter of self-control. Now and then she managed to glance furtively at her husband and wonder why he hadn't flown into a rage; but she was wise enough to say nothing, knowing that as he did not there must be a reason. Nevertheless she mentally resolved to give her young sister such a piece of her mind on their return home as would not easily be forgotten; and for the first time since the date of Jean's early departure had been set, she was reconciled to it. What made matters so very much worse was that Jasper Holt looked distractingly handsome in those unaccustomed white flannels, wearing them as though he had grown up in them, and sitting his mount like a young god. There wasn't a man of the whole line who seemed so thoroughly a part of his horse as Holt, and every line of his head and body, every controlled, easy movement that he made was beautiful. Of course Jean was taken with his looks. Girls were such fools; that is, girls who had no worldly wisdom.

Up on the grandstand a group of girls looked and exclaimed and whispered eagerly together: "Do you suppose Jean knew all the time he was going to enter? Do you suppose maybe she's in love with him? *Really?* Wouldn't that be exciting? But of course it couldn't ever amount to anything but a little romance! And she looks so innocent! I don't believe she knew, after all." And so they speculated.

Jean had known him the first moment he appeared upon the scene and her heart stood still, as if this were the moment for which she had waited all her life. He was here, and

how splendid he looked! The rough flannel shirt and cordu-
roys in which she was accustomed to see him were becoming, but he fairly took her breath away in his new costume.
There wasn't a man among them, no matter what he wore,
who could match him for looks. Her heart swelled with joy
beneath his roses. This was her little moment to rejoice. Tomorrow she was going away, and she might not see him anymore, but today it was right that she should have this
beautiful sight of him to carry away with her. So she
watched, her eyes shining and her cheeks glowing warmly.

There was no question at any time but that he was the
rider of them all. His horse skimmed the hurdles as though
they had been mere imaginary lines, and flew over the highest bar like a swallow in the air. He sat the black creature
with ease and grace, and from the start all eyes were following his every move. The crowd forgot for the time its prejudice and animosity, and sat in absorbed admiration of his
skill and courage.

They all knew him as a daring rider, for often women
held their breath to see him go tearing through the street on
some wild beast of a horse whose mad flight seemed uncanny; but the incomparable riding he did now was beyond
all he had ever done for them before. They watched and
glowed and applauded, and the heart of the girl he loved
swelled with pride so that the tears of joy came into her eyes
and blinded her from seeing him. She was glad that everyone was watching him, and no one would be looking at her.
She did not know that her sister had the field glass focused
straight upon her, and was studying her closely. Alas, for the
tears that were so hastily brushed away. Eleanor looked and
her heart sank in dismay, poor, troubled lady. She began to
rejoice that Jean was going on the morrow; in fact, the afternoon could not come too soon to a close for her now.

The final race, the hardest of them all, intricate and
amazing in its plan and wonderful in its working out, in
which the obstacles were many and the skill required was

great, was at its climax. Holt had kept easily abreast, often ahead of all the others, and the next to the last round was almost finished. People leaned forward in their seats, then rose upon their feet, shouting and cheering and waving their hands. Jean, with the others, leaned over the front rail of the grandstand, in the center of the judges' bench waving her handkerchief excitedly; the bit of sheer linen slipped from her trembling fingers and fluttered to the ground. Quick as a flash, Holt spurred ahead and, wheeling in a circle in front of the judges' stand, swinging his body lithely, he leaned and picked up the bit of linen from the ground, wheeled shortly again and handed it to its owner. Then he was off like a flash down the track on the last round but a quarter of the way behind the rest, his wonderful advantage lost!

"Oh-hh-hhh!" went up in dismay from a hundred throats; and "Ah-hh-h!" in appreciation. It was a pretty bit of gallantry; a skillful trick of horsemanship, but, oh, the pity of it, to lose the race for a handkerchief! The crowd could hardly forgive him. Who cared about all the rest? They were but secondary now even though he had fallen behind. What madness and folly when the handkerchief could have waited, or was he doing it to be smart? The crowd were angry at their sudden loss, and began to think how just like Jasper Holt it was to trifle with them so, when suddenly they sat up and took notice. Was the race lost after all? Jasper Holt had passed the last two riders and was running neck and neck with the third, and now he passed the fourth from the end. There were but two more to pass. Still, the others were nearly to the threequarter line, and the foremost was Captain Wetherill with his powerful roan mare. He was riding hard and meant to win. There was a bitter, haughty look upon his face. His triumph would be spoiled by all that gallery play that had preceded it, though it was plain he felt the victory easy now. Would Holt attempt to pass him? It seemed impossible, yet on he came, his black skimming like a swallow on the outside of the ring, gaining, gaining, every second, and the rider with his easy, nonchalant air, sitting as if the winning was a matter of indifference to him. The crowd stood up and shouted now, a deafening din, and Jean stood with them, holding her breath in wonder and excitement. The man who rode second was but a few paces ahead when his horse suddenly swerved outward, staggered and fell, carrying the rider down with him straight in the track of Holt, coming on at his terrible pace.

The shouting hushed in tightening throats as the crowd waited for the terrible catastrophe that seemed inevitable. Then, before they were fully aware of the danger, the black horse had leaped over the sudden obstacle, and was racing neck and neck with the Captain's horse and gaining every step.

Only fifty yards remained to be run.

Breathlessly the crowd stood and watched as the two leaders sped forward. Would he make it? Would it be possible after all the hindrances for mortal rider to compass that?

The Captain was on his mettle now, spurring his horse to its utmost, but still the black kept easily with him. Like two moats in the sunshine set to swim in unison the racers looked to the excited crowd as they skimmed along together.

Jean clutched the rail in front of her, her eyes blinded once more by sudden tears of excitement, her heart thumping wildly till it seemed as if all those about her must hear it.

Suddenly, incredibly, the black seemed to take on new speed!

A gasp from the crowd, a breath of satisfaction, and then through her tears Jean saw the black leap ahead of his rival and clear the line with a lead of fully ten feet!

Chapter 18

For a moment there was silence, as if the crowd could not grasp the import of the amazing feat it witnessed; as if senses had not yet registered results in human brains. Then a great shout arose, gathering force as it swept along. They stamped, they cheered, they yelled, they waved wild, excited hands with handkerchiefs, umbrellas, canes, anything that was in them. They went mad and prolonged the sound until it was deafening. And there did not seem to be one in that whole crowd who remembered that the man for whom they were shouting had been for years despised by them all.

No one noticed Jean, with her face wreathed in smiles, her eyes sparkling with tears, and her heart beating wildly with joy. She stood on her railed platform, one hand upon her breast to still its excitement, the other hand wiping away her foolish tears which she hoped to get rid of before anybody had time to notice them. It was all so wonderful, so beautiful to her to have her beloved recognized in this way. To be sure, it was only an athletic feat, no recognition of his sterling worth the crowd were giving him in this ovation. She was not deceived. She knew it did not mean any change of their relations; no difference in the circumstances that divided them; but it was something great and beautiful to her to have even his riding recognized thus enthusiastically.

The cheering continued in round after round for several minutes.

Holt had dismounted, halting his horse for a moment, and stood facing the shouting mob, reluctant, yet as if it were something that had to be performed in order to stop their noise. Then with a slight, dignified bow he turned away, and walked toward the fallen rider.

Already a doctor had been called and a crowd was gathering. Holt dispersed them with a wave of his hand and kneeling beside the injured man, began ministering to him with skillful, tender hand, regardless of the shouting of the throng who cheered this new action yet more madly.

The delegation came in hot haste to bring the hero to the judges' stand where Jean, with shining eyes and excited, happy face, stood waiting with the wreath in her hand to crown him, but he paid not the slightest attention to them. Instead he raised a silver whistle to his lips and blew a keen, sweet blast, that even in their excitement startled the crowd and made them remember the tales connected with that whistle and the deeds it had summoned men to do.

Two men jumped down instantly from the front seat of the grandstand and were at his side before the echo of the whistle had died away. Jean saw them and knew them for the men who had ridden out of the woods the day that Scathlin attacked her. They were his special bodyguard, his faithful, tried and true. He sent them off with a word, and in a moment they were back with a hastily improvised stretcher and, lifting the injured man from the ground, bore him away to the tent that had been set up for the use of the ladies. Holt would have followed but for the detaining committee, who laid hands upon him now and insisted eagerly, compellingly, that he was holding up the whole performance and he had no right to spoil the day and keep the lady waiting. Even then Holt might have resisted had they not made mention of the lady, and he looked up and caught her eye and wistful smile—for he had no mind to be further in the public eye. He had ridden for Jean; he wanted not *their* favors.

He took off his hat to her and came forward, and the action touched off the crowd again into a hoarser cry of excitement than before. Someone, madder than the rest, even ventured to bring his name into the cry: "Holt! Holt! Holt! *Hurrah!*"

Holt lifted up his head proudly at that and went forward, not as a man goes who is ashamed before his fellowmen. His bearing was of one who dares to face others, a "gentleman, unafraid." The shout died down in hushed surprise, and then rose on a higher wave that had in it something of the honor and respect his bearing had demanded. And so he came and knelt before her.

In all that wild, excited company only Eleanor Harrington sat unmoved.

"What are they shouting again for?" she asked her husband impatiently. "Isn't this thing almost over? I'm tired."

"They are calling Holt to come to the stand and receive the prize," said Harrington, under his breath, as if it were a bitter thing for him to see.

"How annoying!" said Eleanor, rising to look. "And I suppose Jean will have to present it. If I had foreseen any such thing as this I would have forbidden her to take such a prominent position. I think they have made altogether too much fuss over that creature already. It was an *impertinence* in him to come today and he knew it. He oughtn't to be encouraged. I wonder you didn't take steps to have him put out at the start, James. But, James! There is one thing, Jean *must not* ride around the track with him! I simply *will not have it!* You must go down there quickly and tell her not to. *Forbid* it! Tell her to say she is sick or anything, only she must not ride with him. Quick! Go, James, or it will be too late! She won't have sense enough herself. It will be just like her to think she must, she is so afraid of hurting people's feelings. See, she is standing up with the wreath in her hands. Why don't you go?"

"Hush!" said Harrington, drawing his wife down into her seat again and speaking in a low tone: "Hush! Somebody will hear you. Don't you see she's got to go now? Don't you understand that public opinion will demand it? She'd be a fool to turn back now, she must go the whole show. Besides I can't afford to get his ill-will, and if she didn't go with him Holt would know I had prevented her."

"You can't *afford!*" said his wife angrily. "You can't afford!" and she raised her voice in astonishment and dismay. "What do you mean? I thought you told me only a few days ago that you had him where he couldn't do you any more harm?"

"Hush, Eleanor, haven't you any sense at all? This is no place to discuss business matters. Don't say another word. Things have changed. I had a message from Scathlin. It's all up! Don't mention the matter to Jean, let her ride with him if she likes. I've got to make friends with him somehow or I'm in a bad hole."

Eleanor's face would have been a sight for the neighbors if they had not been too busy shouting to notice.

"Well, I think things have come to a pretty pass if my sister's reputation has to be sacrificed for business," she retorted.

The white, furious look her husband gave her silenced her, however, and she sat back struggling to master her own feelings and understand what her husband had meant.

Dazed and indignant she beheld what was going on at the judges' stand.

Jasper Holt was kneeling almost reverently before the girl whom he had twice saved from death, his bright head bowed, and she, with her eyes all starry bright and a little pink flush stealing into her cheeks, bent and laid the laurel wreath upon his brow.

The crowd hushed its sound while the little ceremony was performed and then shouted aloud again, while Jasper Holt arose and, gracefully as any of the gentlemen assembled could have done it, helped the lady down the steps and to her saddle; then mounting rode beside her, bowing gravely to right and left where were drawn up in line those other contestants over whom he had won his so-great victory. These, in spite of their chagrin, were bowing and smiling graciously, for they would not have the lady know how bitter was their defeat; and so together rode the two, silently, amid the storm of cheers, out into the arena and around the track.

Holt did not presume upon the occasion nor his position to show his intimacy with the girl beside him. Instead he rode with respectful mien, save for one grave, understanding smile at the start, by which she knew how much he hated all this publicity and would have slipped away without it but for her sake. As if their every word and look could have been heard in all that din, they rode with downcast eyes and silent lips, and there was nothing in the whole journey around the course that could in the least offend the watching, anxious, mortified sister.

Not until they were almost back to the judges' stand did Holt attempt to even glance her way, and then he spoke quite low:

"You are going on the morning train?"

She bowed assent because she could not speak. A rush of tears was in her throat at thought of leaving.

"I shall see you again to say good-bye," he said, and gave her one look and smile that filled her heart with joy. Then he left her at the judges' stand with a low bow and rode out of the arena alone; a long, appreciative shout following him out of sight.

Jean, her heart too full for words, watched him; then turned to face her host of friends, who, making the best of their disappointment, were clustering around her and saying pleasant things.

The madness of the crowd over the late hero was dying down even now with his disappearance from the arena. Habit and prejudice were having sway once more. Men laughed deprecatorily over their recent frenzy and said: "Well that certainly was great riding. It takes a daredevil to do the impossible. Of course, we know Holt can ride; still I didn't really think he could do as well as that."

By the time they were out on the street and back in their homes they had recovered their sanity enough to agree with their wives that it was a great piece of impudence for him to ride in and take all the honors away from the men who had worked so hard to make the affair a success. Yet all in their hearts felt again the thrill of excitement as they thought of those last fifty yards of the race, and secretly rejoiced that, impudence or not, Holt had entered the lists.

"You poor little girl," gushed Mrs. Thorne over Jean. "It certainly was a shame that you couldn't have had a more respectable escort in your ride around the track. Of course he looked very well and all that, I wasn't meaning his clothes; and he really behaved much better than I would have expected for him, quite modest, getting out of the way and not presuming at the end. It was so much better than if he had had to be asked to leave, you know, but still, it was a great disappointment that some of your *friends* couldn't have shared the honor with you. Freeman, I know, will be terribly down about not winning."

"Thank you, Mrs. Thorne," said Jean sweetly. "I am sorry your son had to be disappointed, but of course everyone couldn't win, although they all did well, don't you think? But, after all, you know Mr. Holt *is* one of my friends, in fact my first friend, because he saved my life in the wreck when I was on my way here, and helped me to get here. I really felt it quite an honor to ride with him today."

She turned pleasantly to greet the wife of one of the officers from the fort and left poor Mrs. Thorne to gasp and roll her eyes in astonishment. "Of course she doesn't know him; she doesn't understand," said the poor woman in an aside to Eleanor who came up just then. "And perhaps it's just as well she shouldn't as she's going home so soon. Poor Freeman! I don't know what he'll do. He's completely gone over her!"

Then all those fluttering girls came around Jean and began to talk at once.

"Oh, wasn't he simply great! And isn't he handsome in those togs? And isn't it a shame he has to be so wicked? And such a woman hater? I declare I thought he was going to refuse to ride around with you. And, oh, Jean, you sly thing! You knew he was going to enter when you talked about it the other day, didn't you?"

They chattered and buzzed, and the young men came presently and bore them away one at a time. It was the Captain, patient and persevering, who at last, by his very persistence, won the right to ride back to the house by Jean's side. Poor Captain, his last ride, and that glorious smile in her eyes, but not for him!

She was gentle with him when he tried again to persuade her to accept his love. She told him with a wistful sigh that all happiness in this world was not in getting what we wanted, but in knowing things were real and true and fine. She said she should always think of him as her friend, and she hoped he would forget that he had wanted anything else; and she thanked him for his beautiful orchids so sweetly that she left a warm glow in his heart, notwithstanding his double defeat.

Later, as she knelt before her window seat and looked out into the sweet starry night, and over toward the cottage where the Golden Sunset roses grew, she forgot all the petty things that had been bothering her all day, and just let herself be glad for a little while. Then she bowed her head and prayed. "Dear Father, I thank Thee for letting them see so much. Please, some day let them all know him as he really is. Bless him and keep him. I trust him with Thee, dear Lord."

And when she fell asleep at last, weary from the long day and the excitement, against her pillow under her cheek there lay soft cool petals of the golden roses, and their fragrance mingled with her dreams and brought a smile to her lips.

Chapter 19

The breath of the roses on her pillow and the fresh ones on the stand near the bed wakened Jean softly in the early morning, and she lay still, thinking joyously that she was to see Jasper once more before she left. She would have some word, some glance to carry with her on the way. She would have all the beautiful day that was past to put with their other experience together and keep, and she would have that good-bye. It was the knowledge that he had promised to see her again that brought the smile to her lips and the eternal hope of youth to her eyes, when she remembered that this was her last day in Hawk Valley, perhaps forever.

There were not many minutes for such happy thoughts. Her trunk was packed, save a few little things, but they must be put in. The children were already clamoring for her to come downstairs, they could not spare her any longer on this, her last morning.

Before she was entirely ready to go down people began to come to the house to say good-bye and attend her to the station, and when she was finally ready she had gathered quite an escort so that her going through the street seemed quite like a little triumphal procession, a fit continuation of the festivities of the day before.

Eleanor was proud and pleased and weeping all in one, and there was laughing and chatter and banter and many invitations for her to return.

There had been more flowers sent this morning, and boxes of candy and books for her to read on the way. Just before she had left the house Eleanor brought to her more orchids that the Captain had sent, and begged her to wear them just this one last time, but she was already wearing a glorious mass of fresh Golden Sunset roses that she had saved at home the day before for this purpose. Eleanor tried to make her take them off, but Harrington interfered unexpectedly.

"What do you do that for?" he said. "It's all right if she wants to wear them. People will sort of expect it. It's a piece of her triumph of yesterday. It won't do her any harm."

Jean looked up surprised, caught a shifty, uneasy glance in her brother-in-law's eye, and read his mean, cringing little soul. He would sacrifice her readily to his worst enemy if it suited his needs; she had always felt it—now she *knew* it. He colored under her glance, and tried to affect an air of family concern, but Jean was not deceived.

The train was twenty minutes late. There was laughter and chatter and a renewal of yesterday's merriment around the station while they waited. Jean was enthroned on a pile of packing cases with her flowers about her like some queen, and her admirers at her feet. But though her eyes searched the landscape in every direction, from her vantage height, she could nowhere see Holt, and when the train at last was sighted, a mere speck down the track, she felt her heart sinking in dismay. He had promised and he had not come! It seemed as though she could not go without that last look from his eyes that she had known would be there for her, the convenant for the lonely future.

She tried to smile at the last and say all the bright things that were expected of her, but she could not keep her eyes away from the road that led to Holt's house. When the train finally pulled out, amid the waving multitude of friends and the shouting of last messages and fond good-byes, the tears sprang into her eyes unbidden and dimmed the faces of those on the platform into a great blur.

"Well, I'm glad she's safely off," sighed Eleanor, climbing into the car beside the children, "and I must say that man behaved pretty well not to come down to the train. I didn't think he had that much sense!"

But her husband answered not a word. He drove his car

with grim silence. He was wishing Holt had come, and wondering if his absence portended evil for himself.

The travelers on the eastern express watched with delight the beautiful girl surrounded by her bank of flowers who had come to brighten the monotony of their long trip. They wondered where she was going, and if she had left a beau behind, that she wiped the tears away furtively and kept her head turned, looking out of the window at the landscape, which she could not see for tears.

Captain Wetherill had assumed the care of putting Jean on the train, and had turned over a seat, giving her plenty of room to pile the flowers the other men brought on board, in the empty seat. She seemed like a young queen in her garden, with roses and lilies and violets all about her; but at none of them did she look. Her lips were touching the petals of the golden rose on her breast and her thoughts were with its giver. His fine bearing as he skimmed the ground on his black steed, the touch of his soft, bright hair as she laid the wreath on his brow, the look of homage in his eyes as he raised her hand and led her to her horse, the thrill of his voice when he promised to see her again to say good-bye; and then the leaden fact that he had not come! Over and over she went the round and always came back to that, with the choke in her throat and the tears in her eyes. Excuse after excuse for his not coming were conjured in her mind and rejected; and vague fear for his safety mingled with them too. But the fact remained—he had not—and now she would see him no more!

She tried again and again to gather herself together, and finally succeeded in mastering the tears so that there was only a bright suspicion of them in her eyes, but the sense of sadness and something dear, unfinished and now impossible, pervaded her entire thoughts.

Fifty miles from Hawk Valley the train came to a halt at a tiny flag station, and a young man entered, tall, handsome, eager, wearing a dark blue suit and a soft Panama hat—a perfect gentleman in every detail, a light in his eyes and a smile of welcome on his lips.

Jean did not look up until he was almost beside her seat, and then her heart leaped with a light of welcome in her eyes, when she saw that it was Holt!

With a soft little cry she hustled the overflow of flowers that lay on the seat beside her to the opposite one and made room for him. The others in the car looked and were satisfied. Her beau had not been left behind after all, and he was good to look upon. All was as it should be. They settled back to watch the world-old look on the two young faces, with a contentment and zest that never flags for the sweetest story of all. And there were no unkind critics here, for none of them had ever heard of Jasper Holt.

In the still dark of the evening before, Holt had ridden forth in the opposite direction from that he intended to take, and skirting the town in a wide trail well known to himself, he had taken his way across country to the little flag station, where he left his horse to be cared for until he should return.

Very quietly they sat together, after the first wonderful greetings, and talked. There was over them the sadness of a coming separation which each felt might be forever; and they spoke no word of hope that it might be otherwise. The day before them was a precious treasure they meant to have and keep for life. Many things they learned in that brief time, of each other's hopes, longings and desires. Quietly Holt drew from her many thoughts of her own pure heart wherewith to build his ideal for the future.

Once he looked meaningfully at the great bank of flowers before him and then down at the golden roses on her gown. They did not need to talk much about such things, for their eyes could say it all, and Holt read thoughts quickly, keenly, and spoke the language of a glance to perfection. The words that he felt he had not a right to speak she might read in his face if she chose.

And she chose.

Once, as the afternoon was drawing to a close, he said suddenly, "Harrington sent the papers back to me last evening."

Jean looked up startled, questioning, and met amusement in Holt's eyes.

"He didn't dare to keep them. He professes that he sent them the minute he knew I was at home, and that he has been much disturbed by their presence in his house lest his possession of them might be misunderstood by me."

A little cloud of apprehension came into Jean's eyes.

"Don't be afraid to trust me," Holt said softly, with gentleness in his eyes. "I'm not going to make any trouble for your sister. You know that."

Then a great light of joy came into her face, and the tears which had caused her so much annoyance earlier in the day came rushing back for very joy.

It was in the late afternoon that they reached the city where Jean was to change to the sleeper.

Holt gathered up the flowers to take with her, but she put out a protesting hand.

"Oh, please, I don't want any of them but these," and she laid her hand tenderly over the golden roses at her waist.

A look of love and appreciation came into Holt's eyes, and he dropped the flowers quite happily, to gather up her suitcase and umbrella.

"Let the brakeman take them home to his wife, then," he said joyously.

He left her, at last, in the sleeper, and as he stood beside the train until it moved out of the station, their eyes made promises of trust and loyalty long after their lips were forced to remain silent.

Jean did not weep when she saw the last glimpse of his splendid figure on the dim station platform. She had entered upon her desert, but she had the light of his look to shine in her heart, and her courage rose. Her eyes were bright and undaunted. No tears should break her down now. He had kept tryst and she was content. He would be true and she would trust him always, even if she never saw him again.

Just what the future would hold for her she did not care to think. This strange vow she had made with a man she could not hope to marry with her parents' consent, and whom she would not marry without, she had made on trust and on trust she would keep it.

She did not mean to trouble her dear ones with the story. They had been far away and they could not understand. She would not have them looking at her pityingly, nor thinking of him unworthily. She would trust and live her life, and know that somewhere, somehow he was being true also.

Most unpractical, of course, but dear and ideal. Her sister Eleanor would have said it was foolish, and been glad it was no worse, hoping, of course, that now when she saw no more of him she would get over it very soon. But Jean was not made like that. She knew the heartache that was before her, and knowing, dared to rejoice in it.

Chapter 20

Three days later Jasper Holt rode into Hawk Valley from a westerly direction, serious and silent, with a light of purpose in his eyes and a new dignity about him; and Harrington, meeting him in trepidation, was surprised and not a little disturbed by the steady look of understanding that accompanied the grave bow he gave him.

The tournament had accomplished one thing in Holt's favor, for many men meeting him now acknowledged his presence by a formal greeting who had formerly been wont to ignore him utterly or treat him with contempt. A few even went so far as to try to talk with him in a friendly way when they met him in the post office, though perhaps there was the least bit of condescension about their manner when they did it. But Jasper Holt held on his reserved way, mingling little with any save his chosen few, and presuming not at all on his popularity on the day of the tournament. That incident was closed and he wished it to be as if it were not so far as they were concerned. The greetings of his fellowmen he answered coolly, almost curtly, always briefly, and was gone. Would-be friends found little encouragement in any advances they made. A recognition won by mere physical skill was not what he desired. His pride lay not in that direction. There were things he intended to do, but they would take time, and meantime he went on his independent way and men saw little of him.

Time passed on and Jean's languishing beaux recovered from their various heartbreaks. Other maidens visited Hawk Valley and were feasted and feted and cherished with flowers and tournaments; but Jasper Holt came no more to dispute their victories. He was keeping on his quiet, steady way, and gaining their respect every day.

Not a word passed between Holt and the girl in the east whom he loved. Eleanor never mentioned him in her letters, although her conscience hurt her now and then that she did not; for she was an honest woman and like to given even the devil his due. Moreover Harrington, after a period of restlessness and unstrung nerves, appeared to have settled down to the fact that his enemy was not going to bring him to justice, and had developed a most extraordinary way of saying pleasant things about him now and then. He even suggested once that Eleanor include him in a dinner they were giving for business purposes; but his wife promptly vetoed the idea. Even for business purposes she would not lay aside her principles, she said, and shut her lips in a firm line that reminded Harrington of her younger sister.

Jean in her quiet, safe home had not expected letters from Holt and so had nothing to be disappointed about; but sometimes when her sister's letters came she listened eagerly, hoping for just some little word that would tell her how he was faring; and after they were read she would invariably sit looking wistfully off out of the window. Her father and mother noticed it and wondered if she had left her heart behind her with any of the many young men of whom Eleanor had written. They talked it over at dusk sometimes when they were alone, and looked ahead to the years when their girl would be without them.

"I'd like her to find a strong, noble man," said her father. "I cannot bear to think of her treading her years alone. And yet, here there are very few men of that kind," and he sighed.

"Perhaps we ought to send her back to Eleanor's for another visit," suggested her mother anxiously. "We called her home so soon before her visit was done you know. It may be there was someone there. It may be she would like to go."

Yet when they suggested it to Jean, although her face lighted wistfully she shook her head.

"No, Mother dear," she said firmly, "I'm going to stay with you. I'm not going off there again to get my head turned," and from that purpose they could not turn her, although they tried more than once. So they settled back relieved and happy that she was content to stay with them.

Nevertheless, although she would not go, she cried her heart out that night with longing; yet knew it was better that she should stay.

A year and more had passed with Jean continuing on her quiet way in the home and church. It was not an unhappy place to be. The manse in which they lived was beautiful for situation, built of stone with pretty rooms and many windows, the rooms all cheerful and light and everything pleasant in a simple, unpretentious way. The people of the church loved Jean as they loved her father and mother, and she was welcome everywhere in all the merrymakings. She had a large Sunday school class in the church and another in a mission in the lower part of the town, and her boys were her most devoted followers.

Neither was she without older admirers, for all the young men in the church and neighborhood were her friends, and she was as popular at home as she had been in the west. The little manse reception room was never for long unadorned with flowers of some kind that had been sent to her, and she was never without an escort to anything she cared to attend. Yet, though she had a pleasant circle of young friends and seemed to enjoy their company moderately, she never was deeply interested in any of them; and one by one, those who had tried their fortune at her hand went sadly away and seldom came anymore.

Jean seemed happy. She spent much time with her music and her books, when she was not actually busy about the house or in the parish helping her father with some plan for his poor people or his sick people. But she was growing thin, and the wistful look was ever in her eyes now. Her mother watched her anxiously and was more attentive every day, and her father sighed and wished he could afford to take her off on a foreign trip for a little while. Jean only smiled, and went on her way, doing every day the duty that came next.

Sometimes the longing to hear from Holt grew intolerable. Sometimes she almost yielded to her mother's suggestion that she make Eleanor another visit; but something always held her back. What was she waiting for? A sign from Holt? No, that would probably never come. He had said he was unworthy, and he would not of himself cross her path again. But she could not go after him. He might have forgotten, yet she believed in her heart he had not. Her faith in him glowed bright as ever. Even when her common sense got to work and told her he was but human and by this time the incident of their days together was a thing of the past to him and she ought to be satisfied if her influence had helped him even for a time to let people know the good that was in him; still she did not believe that he had forgotten. She believed he was doing just what he had promised to do, and she must stay here and trust him. At least, if he had forgotten, she would rather never know.

So she lived her life, and struggled with her heartache, and when the pain was too much she knelt and prayed for him she loved. Then at last one day there came a great, fat letter from Eleanor, addressed to Jean. Most of Eleanor's letters were addressed to their mother, so that when Jean took this one from the post office she caught her breath and her heart beat a trifle faster than usual. What could Eleanor have to say to make such a nice, thick letter, and why was it sent to her instead of to Mother? Perhaps she was worried about Mother, or perhaps she wanted to tell some trouble to her and not worry their parents. But always when a letter came from her sister, she felt there was that blessed chance that perhaps she might say some little word about Holt, just to let her know he was alive. It was foolish, of course, because she never had done so, and yet hope is a subtle thing and often abides without reason for its hiding and springs forth at the least encouragement. Then, there was always a little comfort that she said nothing against him, for she knew

that Eleanor was so constituted that if Holt had done anything which the town considered very atrocious Jean would
have had to hear of it within the next twenty-four hours; for
Eleanor liked to establish her theories by facts even if it were
years after they were uttered.

Jean did not open her letter at the office. Her hand was
trembling too much and her heart beating too wildly. She
did not wish to have anyone watch her while she read that
letter, for she had a feeling that her face might tell its secrets
when she was off guard, reading. So she held the letter with
a firm little grip and walked down the leaf-strewn street
among the falling golden foliage, trying to grow calm, and
remember that this was probably just a regular commonplace letter about everyday affairs and nothing unusual in it
at all; and she must not be disappointed nor expect anything
great.

She did not open the letter until she was safe on the vine-
covered piazza at home, sitting in the hammock where she
would not be disturbed. Some strange power held her from
taking it to her mother and sharing its first reading with her
as she usually did any letters she received, especially one of
Eleanor's. Afterward she wondered at this; wondered too, as
she remembered how cold her hand had been, and how it
had trembled when she tried to open the envelope with her
hat pin. She was so agitated, so sure by this time that something was the matter, that as she took the folded sheets from
the envelope she closed her eyes and breathed a quick petition: "Oh, dear Father, make me strong for whatever it is."

Then she unfolded the thick sheets and read the letter.

Chapter 21

"Dear Little Sister:

"I have a strange task before me, to tell you of the fineness and greatness and goodness of a man I once told you was not good enough to save your life. I feel as if I must ask your forgiveness and his. You were keener sighted than we all and we are ashamed!

"Jean what will you say when I tell you that Jasper Holt lies in our guest chamber, your old room—*dying*, I am afraid? And that we have him to thank that our precious baby did not die a horrible death?

"Let me go back and tell you the whole story.

"After you went away James had the most extraordinary change of mind about Jasper Holt I ever saw in him. He just turned right around and began to talk in his favor, even wanted me to invite him to dinner once. It was some business, of course, that he thought he could help him in; but he really got to liking him a little I could see. I suppose it was that tournament and his riding so well; though I never could understand why men make so much of sports. But after it happened you didn't hear nearly so many people talking against Jasper Holt. I think, too, your being so good as to ride around the track with him had something to do with it. People saw you were not ashamed and they had a good look at him and saw the possibilities. They say he was asked, yes, just actually begged, to come in the next tournament and ride, but he wouldn't do it. He hasn't appeared that way since you left. He just went about his business gravely, and everybody began to have a lot of respect for him. They say he has done a lot of good to those men he has living on his place, and they simply worship him. Somebody told James there wasn't one of them but would give his life for him any day. Well, that's something, of course. Strange we never heard about it before. Why, people used to be actually afraid of him and his men. But he has been doing some splendid things here lately. When Mr. Whateley died, just before the harvest, and Mrs. Whateley was left to look after her five little children he took his full force of men over to her place and harvested everything and fixed up things a great deal better than they were ever fixed up before, for Mr. Whateley wasn't much of a manager. And when Lucy Whitcorn was lost for three days he organized his men and went out and searched till he found her. They took hold of hands and marched across country, through the wheat fields, over every spot so they couldn't miss her; and her grandmother just put her arms around Jasper Holt's neck and cried and kissed him when he brought Lucy back asleep in his arms.

"But the greatest thing was when he made the raid on the saloons. You remember Slosson's and The Three Geese? They used to have terrible carouses there. Slosson built a concert room over his saloon, and advertised—had balls and dinners there. The Three Geese got a moving picture show over their place; and between them they made a pretty fair imitation of the bottomless pit in Hawk Valley for a while. People got together and talked about it, and said something ought to be done to stop it, and Sallie White even started a petition about it and got some people to sign but it was near election and no one dared do much. Then one night when things were at their height, and there had been a shooting affair or two, we heard the silver whistle of Jasper Holt's men, and the whole cavalcade of them cantered by on horseback. They went like a streak on their dark horses and they rode straight up to The Three Geese and dismounted. Before anybody knew what was happening they had marched into the barroom and the concert hall and taken possession. They handcuffed everybody in the place and bound them, men and women, and then they set to work and emptied out all the liquor and turned the big fire hose into every room till there wasn't a smell of whiskey left, and it was cleaner than it ever was since it was built. They went to Slosson's and did the same thing. Slosson and Craven of The Three Geese, they put into jail, and some of the others who had been most criminal, and they cleaned the whole place out. Jasper Holt took some of the prisoners to his own house and kept them there till he reformed them, and he has been keeping an eye on them right along ever since. Of course after that, people rallied around him and were only too glad to be counted in with him. They all admired his nerve, and they saw he could make things go, so they turned to work and last month they made him mayor of the town, and he has reformed everything in the place, till you wouldn't know it for the same town. Now, that's the preface and I ought to have told you long ago, little sister, but I suppose I was ashamed to, after all I had said.

"But now I'm coming to the real story, the one that brings the tears to my eyes and makes me feel like sobbing; and I have to stop writing and go and kiss my baby before I can go on.

"This morning (it seems a week ago) I sat at my desk writing my paper for the next club meeting. Baby was out in the yard in his white rompers and his little white hat, with his new red cart that James brought him from Chicago on his last trip. The window was open and I could see him gathering leaves and carrying them in his cart to the sidewalk, where he dumped them in a pile at the edge of the road. I had been having a terrible search for a word in the dictionary, and when I looked up again I saw baby standing out in the middle of the road working away with all his might to back up his cart, the way he saw the big carts do, and dump his leaves on the outside of the pile. I didn't think much about it, because there are no teams around in the early morning usually, and the autos, the few we have in town, don't come on this street much; but just as I was beginning to write again I heard a horrible roaring sound, and horse's feet flying down the street. Something gripped my throat with fear and I could scarcely get out of my chair. I could see the baby standing perfectly still, looking at something coming toward him. His little red wagon was standing on end, the red paint gleaming in the sun. Then I heard that roar again and I called to Jamie to come in quickly, but he didn't seem to know just what to do. He took hold of the handle of his cart and seemed to be worried for fear it would be run over. He tried to hurry with it onto the sidewalk, but being on end it wouldn't work quickly. On came that terrible roar! I don't know how I got out on the porch, but there I saw a great, angry bull bearing down straight upon the baby. I screamed and tried to run down the steps, but I was so frightened my knees just sank under me, and there I was in a heap on the steps struggling to get up, and my baby standing still, not ten feet from the snorting, fiery creature, with its horns lowered at him. I shut my eyes, it was so terrible, like a nightmare, you know, when you can't do a thing. I thought I was going to faint, and I tried to call James, though I knew he wasn't at home. Then a wonderful thing happened. A horse was flying down the street from the opposite direction, straight at the bull, but baby was between. I hadn't time to think before the man on the horse swung over from his saddle, gathered up the baby and dashed sideways out of the bull's way. It was Jasper Holt, and he picked up Jamie just as he did your handkerchief that day at the tournament. The poor little mite held on to his dear red cart handle till he was up in the saddle hindering the horse's movements, of course, and it dangled for a minute right in front of the infuriated bull's eyes, who charged at it viciously. Then the weight of the cart wrenched it from Jamie's hand, and it fell clattering under the horse's feet, but the bull turned and made for the horse, who dashed back and forth from side to side, dodging those awful horns as if he were a human being and knew how to reason. Jasper Holt tried to get near the fence to drop the baby over, but every time he came near the bull was in the way. It was only a second of time that it all took of course, but it seemed hours; and I could only scream, but the bull roared so loud that I couldn't be heard. Then the dear black horse plunged right over the bull and started down the street; but the bull turned and caught him in the thigh with his horn and tore a great gash—oh, Jean, I can't describe it all! It makes me faint even to think of it again. The horse stumbled on bravely for a few paces, but you could see he hadn't a chance with the bull anymore for he was crippled, and Jasper Holt saw it, too.

"By that time some men had come with guns, and that splendid fellow, with the horse staggering under him and the bull charging straight at him, held the baby up in the air and told the men to shoot. It meant a terrible risk to himself, of course, because he was in the line of fire. But there was nothing else to do. They shot as carefully as they could, and in a minute or two the bull gave one awful roar and lurched back. The horse sank, too, and someone took the baby. It is all confusion in my mind. I don't really know what happened, only that after I got Jamie in my arms and hugged him and kissed him till he cried, I looked up and saw them bringing Jasper Holt in at the gate. His eyes were shut and one arm hung at the side. They said he had been shot, but had held up the baby till the bull was out of the fight.

"I made them take him to your room, and someone brought the doctor almost at once, but it was a serious thing, I could see from the first. They wouldn't let me in the room. I telephoned for James, and put the baby to sleep, for he was all worn out with the excitement, and kept starting awake and crying out, 'Naughty cow! Naughty cow!' but just as I laid him down in his crib the doctor came and said Jasper Holt wanted to see me.

"Jean, I didn't think a few minutes could make a differ-

ence like that in a great, big, strong man. He lay there so still
I thought he was dead at first; and white under all his fine
tan. He was white as a ghost, with his head all done up in
bandages and his beautiful hair clotted with blood, for one
of the shots plowed deep into the scalp, it seems. He opened
his eyes—what wonderful eyes he has!—and looked at me as
if he were pinning his last hope upon me, and he smiled just
faintly. I never knew what perfect lips and teeth he had before—and his smile just like a little child's!

"One could see it was a great effort for him to speak.

" 'Will you tell your sister that I've kept my promise?' he
said, slowly and distinctly.

"When I told him I would, his eyes lighted up, as if the
sun were shining behind them, and then they fell shut and I
think he must have fainted again. I came quite close and
tried to tell him how grateful I was to him for saving the
baby's life, but his eyelids never even quivered. Then the
doctor drew me away and said it wasn't any use to talk, that
he couldn't hear me, so I came away, but I couldn't do a
thing but just hover around the door till James came. Then
he went in and found out how things were. It seems the bull
gored him. They call it a 'scratch,' but by their faces I know
it's a pretty serious scratch.

"Three shots entered his body, one a deep scalp wound,
one in his shoulder, and one in his arm. They have been
probing the wound and having some kind of an operation.
They don't know whether he will pull through or not. They
say the only thing that is in his favor is his splendid health.
The men are talking now about his fine clean life, and way
he has been doing lately, especially. It seems he never drank
nor did a lot of things that people took for granted he did.
Oh, Jean, I can't stand it if he doesn't get well so I can thank
him for saving my baby for me. To think that if it weren't
for him lying there dying now I should have nothing left of
my beautiful baby but a little mangled corpse!

"Jean, I know now why you looked that way when you

said I did not know Jasper Holt—the fine, true, strong, brave, tender. . . ."

But the tears blinded Jean's eyes and she could read no more. For a moment she bent her head and sobbed behind the vines. But only for a moment. A frenzy of fear seized her. He was dying perhaps, and he needed her!

She lifted her head with sudden resolve and hastily read the closing sentences of the letter. Then, gathering up the scattered sheets, she hurried to her father.

Chapter 22

"Father!" said Jean, closing the study door and standing guard in front of it lest her mother enter suddenly and be frightened at what she was saying, "Father, I must go to Hawk Valley at once—today! No, it isn't Eleanor, nor any of them," she added hastily, as she saw the quick apprehension in her father's face. "They are all well. I've just had a long letter from Eleanor. Father, it's the man who saved my life! He is dying and he needs me. I know he wants me. I love him, Father, and he loves me! He didn't think you would like him, and so we never said anything about it. But now he's dying and I *must go!*"

The look in her eyes and the tilt of her chin were her father's own when he felt he must fulfill some high calling and would not be gainsaid. He knew at a glance that it was useless to try to stop her. Besides, he had all confidence in her.

"I see, daughter," he said with instant comprehension and a swift vision of what the wistfulness in her face had meant all these long months. "How soon can you be ready? There is a train at six, I think."

"I will be ready, Father," she said, and then, turning laid her head for an instant on his shoulder and hid her face in his neck. "Oh, Father *dear!*"

He folded her close and kissed her. "Courage, daughter! Trust in our Father's tenderness."

"Thank you so much, Father, for understanding," she said, lifting her eyes to his face.

"You will want me to go with you, daughter?" he asked, trying to think how it would be possible.

"No, Father, you couldn't. You have that funeral tomorrow, and they need you," she answered, drying her tears.

"And then, it wouldn't do to leave Mother. No, I can go alone perfectly well. Here is Eleanor's letter. Read it with Mother. That will explain a good deal. I will tell you more on the way to the station. He is the one who won the laurel wreath at the tournament. I told you a little about him. . . ."

"Yes, I know. I understand! Poor little child! Now go quickly and I will explain to your mother about it. You haven't much time. Don't try to pack more than a suitcase. We can send your trunk on after you."

There are not many fathers so wise as this one, who seemed to know without asking just what was needed, who refrained from needless questions, calmed the frail mother's fears, and helped his girl away to her pain or her rejoicing as it should prove to be, with a blessing upon her as she left.

It was in the sunset gloaming that she arrived in Hawk Valley and the gold of the sky lay behind the hills, ruby lined, like the gold of Jasper Holt's roses whose sweet withered leaves lay stored among her linen in her bureau drawer at home.

They met her at the station, for a telegram had heralded her coming. Quietly, with hushed voices, they met her; for death waited beside the couch in the guest room of their home, and they had guessed how it must be between these two.

"He seems to be sleeping his life away," said Eleanor, folding a cloak about her sister, for she saw that it was going hard with her. "They cannot rouse him. He seems content to go. He does not want to live. It is strange with one so strong and young. . . ."

The light of battle came into the younger sister's eyes, but she answered nothing.

"Better come and get something to eat first," said Eleanor, when they reached the house, but Jean shook her head and fled up the stairs.

There could not have been anything quieter than the way she opened the door and slipped into that room. Her very garments seemed to cling and hush about her as she walked. But he opened his eyes at once; a strange, wondering look came into them as she came across the room and knelt beside him with a smile. Then she bowed her head and laid her lips upon his.

The doctors and the nurse who stood by were as nothing. There were just these two in the universe and all else was hushed.

So she moved about his room, or sat close beside his couch. She was there when he woke in the night and looked at her, murmuring very low:

"Are you real or a dream?"

"I'm real, dear. I will not go away," she breathed, and laid her soft lips on his again. This time his own responded feebly.

It was in the morning that the doctors said there was hope, though they confessed afterward that recovery began with his first sight of Jean's face.

Jean scarcely left his side day or night, and seemed tireless. Often she slept on a low stool beside the bed, with her head against his pillow. One bright morning he awoke to find her sleeping so, and laid his weak, uncertain hand softly upon her head. She opened her eyes, met his smile, and knew that he was better.

"A life for a life," he said softly. "Dear, you must go to your bed and rest. I will get well now. You are killing yourself."

But her smile shone forth radiantly.

"I couldn't rest away from you," she said, giving him a dazzling look. "I'm not going to leave you anymore, ever!" Then she paused and looked shyly up again. "Unless," she added archly, "unless you've changed your mind and don't want me. In that case I'll go back home as soon as you are able to be out."

"Oh, *my dear!*" he said softly, and drew her down to his breast with his one good arm. "Do you mean it? Not leave me again ever? Are you willing to be my wife? Can you really trust me now?"

"I've trusted you always," she said softly, nestling her face against his cheek. "I trusted you the first time I saw you."

"But your people, Jean?"

"My people all love you and honor you," said Jean, with shining eyes. "They think you are magnificent! They cannot say enough about you. Eleanor would bow down and kiss your feet, and my father and mother know all about you and have sent me to you willingly. But, Jasper, listen, if everyone in this wide world were against you, even my dear people, I should marry you anyway and stay with you! I couldn't live any longer without you!"

He looked into her eyes, and he drank in her trust and loveliness, and beautiful self-surrender as if it had been some life-giving draught; then he laid his hand upon her hair and pressed her closer to him.

"Oh, you wonderful woman!" he said.

It did not take Jasper Holt long to get well after that. Hope and joy shone in his eyes so that his face was dazzling to look upon, and those who came into his room walked softly, filled with awe, that a man who had come and gone among them for years and been held almost in contempt could have within him a soul so great and noble as to shine like that in his face.

Jean's father and mother came west for a visit about that time, for Jean wrote that there was no use expecting her to return now, and when the two met, Jean's father and Jasper, and stood hand in hand, looking into each other's eyes for a full, long minute before either spoke, each felt entirely satisfied.

Of course all this could not go on without the town knowing something of the state of things, for everybody came to find out how the hero was getting on; and Jasper Holt's men, as they came and went in grave concern, were beset with questions. And when Jean arrived, then her parents, the town opened eyes of understanding and nodded gravely, thinking it was well.

So when it was announced most informally that a wedding would take place no one was surprised. Indeed, Jean's girl friends had been embroidering and chattering away over wedding gifts for a week before it was whispered officially that they would be needed.

Once more the Harrington house was smothered in flowers for Jean. Gifts came from far and near, from all her old admirers who were now also with one consent become Holt's admirers. But the flowers that Jean carried in her arms when she came down the stairs, white clad and smiling, to meet her bridegroom, were great Golden Sunset roses, gathered by Holt's faithful men for her; and among the guests were all those men, fifty-four of them, standing grim and embarrassed outside the door to watch their leader stand among the flowers and take his beautiful girl bride by the hand.

It was sunset again, gold and ruby sunset, when they went home to his house, after the wedding supper.

The sky was broad and clear translucent gold, with a deep heart of pure ruby blazing out behind the rose-wreathed cottage when Jean saw it for the first time. The roses hung in heavy-headed wealth about the doorway, and the men stood double ranked each side of the path. They had decked the house for her coming, those rough men who loved her lord, with boughs of sweet-smelling branches; heaped up blazing logs in the big stone fireplace, and sand-strewn the floor all clean and fresh. There alone at last together in their own home they stood with ruby and golden light from the sunset windows mingling with the soft flicker of firelight, and looked into each other's eyes and knew that their heavenly Father had been good to them.